…三二部曲

地下女子

Underground
Women-Paradise Lost

鍾伯淵 著

目錄
CONTENTS

推薦序　除了想像，只能無言的銘記！

文／于善祿（臺北藝術大學戲劇學系助理教授）

劇本的最開頭，舞台指示就寫著，除了序曲及終章之外，其餘的十五個段落可以由演員在演出的當下，隨機排列演出的場序，那等於至少有「15的階乘」種排列組合的方式，一般的電子計算機可能是算不出來的，我在計算紙上，土法鍊鋼，將15乘以14，再乘以13，再乘以12，……，一直到乘以1，最後得出的乘積是13105546080000，一兆三千多億，已經是個天文數字了。

對我而言，這表示這個劇本已經自成一個世界，不論從什麼樣的結構順序去閱讀、理解，都跑不出這個地下社會世界的手掌心，這種寫作技巧，有點像意識流，也有點像美術史上的立體派或郎靜山的「集錦攝影」，當然它肯定是後現代、後結構，甚至是新文本的自由拼貼與組裝。

透過如此多焦、零碎、片段、彌散的書寫，那地下社會呈現出一副何等的景觀呢？

在創作者的筆下，那似乎是個陽光和煦、微風飄香、結實纍纍的天堂極樂淨土與應許之地，但那其實只是地底人想望與期待的假象；真實的情況反倒是生活貧瘠，日子難挨，縱使有繁花盛開、綠草如茵的谷地，卻是危險的，他們被困陷在進退、上下皆不得的逆境之中，甚至被警告（教育）不可擅自離開。挑明了說的話，那其實是個佔地廣大的集中營區，櫛比鱗次，地底人不但要承受著莫名消失與死亡的恐懼，還要為了搶奪少量的食物配給、為了存活下去，而相互地殘殺，所謂「自己的飯菜自己救」（挪借嫁接了近年台灣公民行動常見的精神口號：「自己的國家自己救」）。

地下女子

004

在這樣惡劣的存活環境中，當地的長老還留下了三道明訓：「不可爭執，不可憤怒，不可離間」，很明顯，這是對於摩西十誡的仿借，然而放在地底集中營的情境下來理解，這其實是明哲保身的三句箴言；連碧娜的媽媽都不斷地教導、告誡自己的女兒，做人不要衝太前面，以免太招搖惹禍，也別落後太多，以免遭到淘汰，盡量維持在中間平庸就好，能夠安身保命就好，畢竟「棒打出頭鳥」。完全可以體會，作為一名母親，而且是集中營裡的母親，經歷過多少死難離別的場面，所能夠教給女兒的，只能是如此微弱的耳提面命，日子再艱難，只要能夠存活下去就好。

這些明訓箴言與耳提面命，幾乎抑制了地底人的情緒表達與宣洩，太壓抑、太不正常了。這自然是我們事後諸葛的短淺眼光，自以為正義地為地底人吶喊、抱不平；當今許多對於歷史不明不識、無感無知的井底之蛙，只會玩弄歷史、穿越歷史、與歷史切割斷裂的白目之士，又豈能理解（遑論體會）地底人的諸般考量？

如果集中營就是日常，而且是納粹集中營，所能做的，也就只是想辦法存活，但偏偏在納粹集中營裡，什麼時候會面臨死亡，只知道可能不久不遠，但無法確定，而一旦確知了，卻也正邁向死亡，而且極可能是痛苦、非人道的死亡。在集中營裡談選擇是奢望的，無從選擇，抱怨、憤恨也沒有用，只能適應，那幾乎是一種絕望的適應，久而久之，對死亡也麻木而視若無睹了，又能怎樣呢？人也被物化及異化了。這是何等地泯滅人性、文明退化？竟然還有人敬之崇之，甚至是嬉鬧仿之！

在如此經驗匱乏的年代，我們要如何面對？透過網際網路或爆量資訊，絕對能夠輕易地獲知關於飢餓、死亡與毀滅的相關訊息，而且保證圖像、影音、文字並茂，但這又代表什麼？沒有親身體驗，仍不知悲傷與沉痛。

至此，我終於明白劇首序曲舞台指示所謂不需要場次順序的意涵，因為我在閱讀劇本的過程中（至少換了幾種不同的順序），每一場或長或

地下女子

短，但多半都令人感到沉痛而無法言語，直問世間怎麼會有如此的人與事？

真有，曾經在歷史與世界的彼端！我除了想像，真的只能無言的銘記。

創作者不是要展現傷痛與傷痕，而是要誠實地直視與面對，與其說是一個文青或憤青，倒不如說是一位勇敢、有人文深度的知青。我特別對劇中歌者所唱的某段詞句有感，引錄如下，望能點醒嘴砲「鍵」客們，這個世界並不只是你們所想像的那樣：

別說你知道

誰能通達知曉

情感的問答

是非對錯你知了

知識的風暴

……

了解太表面
同感太敷衍
體會太做作
憐憫太倨傲
別說你知道
傷痛只有自己遭遇才明瞭
再多的話都無效
讓你是我　體會我內在的風暴
讓你是我　才不會只是表面的哀悼
如果你知道
不要再說話
就一個擁抱

推薦序 《地下女子》的寓言象徵

文／梁紅玉（資深媒體人）

寓言是一種「寓意於言」的敘事方式，寓是寄託；言是述說，而意則為蘊含其中的道理，換言之，用說故事的輕鬆方式將深奧道理寄於其中，常是劇場裡採用的表現手法。《地下女子》作為「曉劇場」《穢土天堂》系列的二部曲，全劇將主人翁碧娜於死前三日的告白，以十七個短篇隨機串聯，除用以凸顯記憶的支離破碎；或也在呈現虛實交錯的時空。然而，首部曲偏重「文化侵略」下的暴力和權力關係，進而反思社會建構中的種種謊言與神話，二部曲則藉由「象徵寓意」的情節進行辯證。

序場由一縷幽魂的甦醒開始。首部曲中舉槍自盡的阿道夫，還有被遣送回地底世界、瀕臨死亡的碧娜，在「不存在俗事的美妙之地、有一片土地色彩繽紛」的天堂美境展開對話。我以為「眼淚」在此具有某種涵意，人在死前剎那流淚的臨終告別，不同宗教或有不同的解讀，但在戲裡，這一滴屬於懺悔的淚，該由誰的眼睛去流淌？誰又該為這一切災難承擔？

阿：碧娜（拉長地），碧娜妳在那裡？

碧：（只有聲音）我在這裡，快來找我，來找我呀！

阿：我看不到妳。

碧：（只有聲音）就在妳眼角邊，求求妳讓我流下來，找到我，我已

　　經打轉了好久。

不妨隨機抽取幾個片段吧！在「雞與牛」的段落裡，兩隻動物打開話匣子聊起天來，彼此談論的是死亡議題，一隻「歸歸歸，不歸」的雞，每天來來回回走動「找死」；而另一個「哞～～喔」的牛，則不斷反芻咀嚼

在「等死」。

雞：：不歸、不歸；牛有幾種死法？

牛：：（不解地）嗯？

雞：：我們有幾千幾萬隻雞，但只有一種死法。

牛：：了解哞～～。

（雞脖子伸長，雙腳亂踢，接著發出帶有咕嚕和逐漸失去的雞鳴聲，接著像被丟入溫熱水中浮沉，再被拎起丟入脫毛滾筒，雞一邊旋轉一邊自己發出肉身撞擊滾筒控咚控咚的聲響；重覆數次。牛一邊咀嚼一邊觀看。雞作嘔。）

諾貝爾文學獎得主柯慈（J.M.Coelzee），曾在《動物的生命》中，藉著畜牧場的屠宰，探討死亡殺戮的動機與合理性，進而認為「人類容許自己屠殺動物，只因視而不見」。此刻，舞台上雖沒有血肉橫飛的真實場景，但「集體冷漠必然助長暴力」的控訴，卻一再透過冷眼旁觀與文字指涉，鋪天蓋地襲來。即便死亡是一條不歸路，但我們是否應知「死，有重於泰山，也有輕如鴻毛」？最後不免反問碧娜「妳為什麼不逃？」

法農（Frantz Fanon）在《黑皮膚白面具》書中，一再提醒我們：「奴隸並不是用膚色（外觀）來決定，而是由他自卑的、毫無自主的內心來決定」。然而，人並非天生具有奴性，在社會學認知裡，文化具有一種「內化」過程，我們「看待世界的方式、感受事物的方式」以及在群體中與人互動的方式，都是透過學習而來的，但「內化」卻意味著「我們不曾意識到自己的學習歷程」。碧娜的沉默，是否其來有自？

碧：媽！為什麼這時候你又要搬出長老的教條來堵我的嘴。

媽：不可爭執（頓），不可憤怒。

碧：媽媽，我只是很疑惑如果都不去討論前因後果，會進步嗎？

媽：討論也不一定會有進步，做好你自己份內的事。人家說棒打出頭鳥，記住，什麼事情都別衝的太前面，衝太前面只有被打的份，能交由別人決定的事就交給別人；但也別落的太後面，免得被淘汰掉。

雖然「內化」是一種無意識的行為，但，意識到之後呢？終曲中，碧娜呼喊著早已過世的母親：「媽媽，你還沒有告訴我⋯⋯我的最後三日什麼時候會來」，因為有一個傳說：「地下人在死前三日會陷入黑暗之中面對過去，接受早一步離開朋友的祝福；最後通過母神的甬道，被產出在新世界裡」。末尾，背景字幕打出了「聽說碧娜在洞穴深處看到光亮⋯⋯」。

在此引用韋伯（Max Weber）的說法，人類「有意識地行動本身」是極為重要的，因為這說明了我們能夠更「清楚明白」地看待事情的來龍去脈。從《穢土天堂》首部曲裡的質疑，再到二部曲《地下女子》的象徵寓意，我們有幸識得了創作者深刻地用心。

前言

文／鍾伯淵

在我貧窮的幼年記憶裡，想像力是我最好的玩具，不論用白紙剪黏而成的車子和架設的城市和高速公路，用十元一盒、慢慢收集來的機械戰士配對拼湊各種劇情，或是在山上奔跑看樹影搖曳、光影婆娑間有通往異界的神秘通道；夜晚就把椅凳朝上、擺放紙箱並蓋上棉被，建構只能匍匐其中的迷宮；有一陣子，睡眠時就把枕頭、棉被拖到床底看著床板想像自己在漂浮的太空船中沉沉入睡，這些隨機變換的秘密基地讓每個夜晚不再一成不變。

不論是自己的空間或房間，實體場域總能助長思慮、想像向外蔓延，於是當我起筆「地下女子」時，便從僅有碧娜的空間、充滿記憶的場域開始，倘若以此為終點的起點回望自身，又將會覷得何種景致？

從二○一一年開始的累積至二○一三年的動筆一路行至二○一四年初，因為台灣社會劇烈動盪讓我停筆三個月，那段時間我看著友人在抗議現場，被拖行、被毆打，對著鏡頭憤怒；在他方駐留的我僅能全天候開著直播，憂傷並焦慮，有太多的情緒及控訴是我無法寫入劇本內的，那極可能會摧毀掉一個待在自己空間的女人迫使她走出房外，並在洪流中失聲。

唯有等到那情緒再度收束，那女子才能細細爬梳自己的過往。

在劇本中確有台灣事件的影子，但我希望能模糊身影、隱藏其中，因為碧娜自過去、現在和未來都存在，隱藏的符碼留待未來的考究與自身相近的社會背景想互呼應即可，正如同初始將二戰歷史架空建立的世界觀，說明歷史不斷輪迴的苦難。

但我們可能歸結出不再輪迴的頓悟，於是在劇本中除了序曲和終章固定外，中間段落可供演員在每場演出過程中隨機挑選、改變順序，或許在每一次搬演中也能讓演員透過自己感覺與角色產生連動，震盪出更大的能量，讓我們持續不斷透過創作來找到那些閃現的靈光。

《地下女子》

此劇除序場及終曲為最前與最後外，中間所有段落交由演員於每段演出中隨機排列、決定下段演出段落。

角色：

碧娜（牛、老鼠B）

幽魂（阿道夫、母親、莎夏、海倫娜、東洞阿浪、阿姑婆、雞、老鼠A……）

歌手

樂手

場景：

非特定空間，舞台上有一個水池，開場時一個男人浮在水池中。

序場

（開場時，男人從水中爬起。）

幽魂：這裡是哪裡？（停頓）這裡是哪裡？（停頓）妳認得出來嗎？如果妳認得出來就可以告訴我這裡是哪裡，但是妳認得出來嗎？妳想得起來嗎？妳會想起來嗎？妳敢想得起來嗎？妳敢承受嗎？或是妳從來都沒有想起來過？妳在這裡卻沒有想過「我在哪裡？」、「為什麼我在這裡？」或是「這裡到底怎麼了？」。

妳從來都沒有想起過；但我們小心地避免使用「從來」兩個字，「從來」的否決感太強讓人抗拒、讓人否認，

（一人分飾二角）

「我從來都沒有減肥成功。」

「我從來都沒有想認真工作。」

「我從來都沒有喜歡過我老闆。」

「我從來都沒有喜歡過自己。」

「我從來都不喜歡你。」

「真的嗎?」

(停頓。)

「我也從來都沒有喜歡過你。」(極其嚴肅地而後感到強烈的打擊)……,重來!我們要禮貌和緩地說妳「可能」沒有想起過,也覺得沒有什麼好在乎的,因為生活之於妳從來都沒有改變,妳用了光陰荏苒來概括自己多年來的經歷,其實是因為妳再也說不出什麼印象深刻的生活光景了;當然也不用「麻木」這兩個字,那太褻瀆妳確實有過的遭遇和過往的光陰,雖然妳也的確說不出個所以然來,而且麻木本身就讓人感到麻木。這裡是一個陽光和煦、微風披掛著青草的芳香、引動樹木枝葉發出沙沙的聲響(突然地狂風暴雨)中心最大風速來到每小時一五〇公里搭配驚人雨勢，山區每小時可降下破千毫米雨量，請嚴加戒備山洪及土石流警戒……，（音效結束，停頓。）

嗯，……微風，我們說到微風，然後是綠草如茵、廣闊無垠地在眼睛裡開展，劃開草地的清泉，還有結實纍纍的果樹；這就是我們所在的地方……。

（歌曲）〈穢土天堂〉

有一片土地一塵不染

潔淨無瑕噢

鳥兒在樹上悅耳的啼囀

樂音流淌

還有七色雲彩藍天徘徊

天光悠轉

極樂的天堂

有一片土地色彩繽紛

萬紫千紅

蜂蝶紛飛

動物無憂

有一片土地好漂亮

有一片土地好夢幻

有一片土地讓人心生嚮往

心生嚮往

幽魂：可是其實呀，這裡是鯨魚的肚子噢，我們生活在鯨魚的肚子裡；

啊……，好貧瘠的生活呀，我們這樣說，卻只巴望著鯨魚張開嘴巴時

灌進來的食物，（巨大水流聲，男人挑剔地作出撿拾的動作一般發出

噴噴的呷嘴聲。）啊～，又是這些東西呀，真是難捱呀、這可不行呀，啊……的痛苦指數要破表啦，我不能Handle了（做出取出罐子倒藥細數、吞嚥的動作，而後繼續之前的動作。），啊～好痛苦呀，又是這些東西呀，真是難捱呀、我快不行啦，（取出罐子倒藥細數、吞嚥的動作。）啊～好悲慘，又是這些東西呀，真是難捱呀、啊～都out of control啦（再次取出罐子，停頓，直接仰頭全數吃下，委頓在地。）！百般抗拒的寧願躲在鯨魚的肚子裡苟活，是不是？我遭遇患難求……（摀嘴），……就應允我；從陰間的深處呼求，……就俯聽我的聲音。你將我投下深淵，就是海的深處；大水環繞我，你的波浪洪濤都漫過我身。我說：我從你眼前雖被驅逐，我仍要仰望你的聖殿。諸水環繞我，幾乎淹沒我；深淵圍住我；海草纏繞我的頭。我下到山的根部，地的門將我永遠關住。

（歌曲）

這裡是天堂的境地

有最美的景色噢

這裡是一塵不染的美地

沒有罪惡

沒有邪惡

這裡是應許之地

不存在俗世的美妙之地

有一片土地色彩繽紛

萬紫千紅呀

蜂蝶紛飛呀

動物無憂呀

心生嚮往　嚮往呀

阿：（拉長地）碧娜、碧娜妳在哪裡？

碧：（只有聲音）我在這裡，快來找我，來找我呀。

阿：我看不到你。

碧：（只有聲音）就在你眼角邊，求求你讓我流下來，找到我；我已經打轉了好久。

阿：在誰的眼角邊？

（燈光逐漸收暗聚集到阿道夫身上）

碧：（只有聲音）我……。

阿：在誰的眼角邊？

碧：（只有聲音）這個……。

阿：在誰的眼角邊？快告訴我？讓我找到妳呀？

碧：（只有聲音）快來找我。

阿：我會的。

碧：（只有聲音）但為什麼要找到我？

阿：因為妳想離開黑暗。

碧：（只有聲音）對，我想離開黑暗，幫幫我。

阿：我會。

碧：（只有聲音）莎夏呢？她在哪裡？

阿：她已經走了。

（兩具骷髏的區域亮起。）

碧：海倫娜呢？

阿：她也走了。

碧：（只有聲音）她們一起走的嗎？

阿：是的。

碧：（只有聲音）是嗎？她們一起走的嗎？

阿：是的。

（兩個帶著燦爛笑容的女孩出現在後方）

碧：（只有聲音）只留下我嗎？

阿：只有妳。

碧：（只有聲音）還有你在對不對？

阿：（遲疑地）算吧，我在……，妳在哪裡？

碧：（只有聲音）我不知道。

阿：妳剛說妳在誰的眼角邊？我去他旁邊找你。

碧：（只有聲音）我想我在我的眼角邊，流不下來。

（燈暗後隨即亮起）

碧：媽媽，媽媽。

母：怎麼啦？

碧：我出不去。

母：在哪裡出不去？

碧：到處；我陷在一個困境裡，不知道該怎麼辦？我無法做出選擇，可是
又不想不做選擇。

母：如果妳想選擇，就選擇；所有的選擇都可能伴隨錯誤。

碧：我不懂。

（燈光變化）

浪：我是東洞的阿浪！今晚妳想吃炸田雞腿還是清蒸白魚？

碧：嗯？（思索）我都想。

浪：但妳只能選一樣。

碧：炸田雞腿好了。

浪：但今晚的炸田雞腿可能炸得不夠酥脆。

碧：還是清蒸白魚？

浪：也可能白魚太腥太乾？

碧：那我該怎麼辦？

浪：我們好久沒吃白魚了。

碧：對呀。

浪：聽說最近白魚特別肥嫩。

碧：那我們吃白魚好了。

浪：妳是真的想吃白魚，還是我說妳才想吃？

碧：我不清楚。

浪：那吃炸田雞腿好了。

碧：等等，妳不是說要讓我選嗎？

浪：那妳想吃什麼？

碧：我想吃炸田雞腿。

浪：即便炸得不夠酥脆？

碧：嗯。

浪：也可能炸得太油還是調味不夠好？

碧：也沒關係。

（燈光變化）

母：妳做出了決定，即便這決定可能不會帶來妳所想像的美好，而妳依然在分歧點上決定了某個方向，是嗎？說不定今天的白魚會是前所未有的美味，而炸田雞腿會獲得空前的失敗；我們都不知道。

碧：那媽媽妳覺得今晚吃炸田雞腿還是清蒸白魚好呢？

母：今晚只有炒薯根。

碧：噢……。

母：有時候讓妳做了決定，事情也不會往妳要的方向走，說不定兩個方向都不會，而是第三個、第四個，更好的或更壞的。

碧：我不知道該怎麼辦了，站在原地可以嗎？

母：沒有原地，妳會被推著走。

碧：但我不做任何決定。

母：這也是一種決定。我們都在母神的肚子裡，我們只是在母神的肚腹裡等待產出；在此之前我們要不停地反芻是非對錯，把所有來自於情緒的決定都選擇過一次，等到我們做出最純粹的選擇，就會從母神的產道裡走出來，出生在新的世界裡。

碧：媽媽，要怎麼知道何時會做出最純粹的選擇？

母：我也不知道。

碧：我害怕自己等不到這天。

母：不要怕，在選擇之前，早妳一步被母神產下、最親愛的朋友都會回到妳身邊，用三天的時間，最後三天一起和妳重新做一次決定。

碧：我最親愛的朋友會是誰？誰會在最後三天陪在我身旁？（靜默）莎夏，是妳嗎？海倫娜，妳在哪裡？（停頓）媽媽？妳還在嗎？

（沒有任何動靜）

碧：媽媽，妳還沒告訴我最後三天長什麼樣子？（停頓）我一直在等，莎夏？海倫娜？妳們在哪裡？我的最後三天在哪裡？

（歌曲）〈最後三天〉

噢～最後的三天
等自己被圍繞
還有那些過去的
遺憾的和不後悔的
都來眼前
和親愛的朋友一起
把所有的故事重新撿起
在最後的三天
讓自己被決定圍繞

地下女子
034

為了和親愛的朋友

一起被母神在新世界擁抱

它怎麼到

妳還沒告訴我最後的三天

媽媽呀

但是

（燈暗）

間奏　行動句

（下列括號內句子由旁白所說，碧娜亦同時跟隨指令動作。）

（碧娜站在原地。）

（碧娜站在原地。）

（碧娜站在原地。）

（碧娜沒有欲望。）

（碧娜沒有情感。）

（碧娜沒有行動。）

（碧娜沒有思考。）

（碧娜沒有生命。）

碧娜：我還活著。

（碧娜依然活著。）

（碧娜依然等待。）

（碧娜依然麻木。）

（碧娜依然活著。）

（碧娜依然麻木地活著。）

（碧娜依然麻木地活著。）

（碧娜依然麻木地活著並等待。）

（碧娜依然麻木地活著並等待……。）

碧娜：等待死亡的到來。

（碧娜等待死亡的到來。）

（碧娜等待死亡的到來。）

（碧娜等待最後的三日到來。）

（碧娜等待死去母親的到來。）

（碧娜等待死去友人的到來。）

（碧娜等待死去鄰居的到來。）

（碧娜等待死去親戚的到來。）

（碧娜等待死去同學的到來。）

（碧娜等待死去莎夏的到來。）

（碧娜等待死去海倫娜的到來。）

（碧娜等待自己的死亡到來。）

碧娜：碧娜等待自己死亡的到來。

（死亡沒有到來。）

海倫娜

（海倫娜穿著一件蓬蓬紗裙雙腿打開地坐在地上，目光呆滯地將棒狀物往嘴巴裡來回抽送。一邊抽動一邊與碧娜對話。）

海：喔、喔、嗯。

碧：（折著花）含進嘴巴，不要用力；用妳的頭繞圈，當妳轉圈的時候棒子就會在妳嘴裡左右翻轉。

（海倫娜照做，翻轉一陣後。）

海：嗯；姊姊，我頭暈。

碧：妳左右擺動幅度太大了，而且這樣牙齒會刮傷……會吃鞭子的。

海：喔。（停下手邊工作，放空；碧娜看了一陣。）

碧：嘿，怎麼停下來了？真空吸引學會了嗎？

（海倫娜搖頭）

碧：這麼初級的技巧到現在都還沒學會，長官們怎麼會高興呢？（指導著海倫娜）來，淺淺地含入口中，嘴巴吸，對；收縮口腔就會造成真空的效果啦。（海倫娜吸太猛整根棒子沒入口中，反胃。）不，淺淺的；（海倫娜淺淺地含住棒子並吸吮）對，妳總算學會了，就是這樣。

海：我學會了。

（碧娜繼續折花，海倫娜則持續地練習「真空吸引」，開始哼唱歌曲。）

（歌曲）〈轉圈圈〉

轉呀轉呀繞圈圈

把棒棒放在　嘴巴攪一攪

輕輕地搖搖頭晃晃腦

轉太大力　頭會昏昏

要輕輕繞　轉圈圈

還有真～空吸引

哼哼哼　不吃棒棒　就吃鞭子

燙燙辣辣

開一朵花

哼哼哼哼噢～

（海倫娜逐漸顯得沒勁，再次停下動作。）

碧：海倫娜。

海：海倫娜。

海：姊姊；我想吃烤地鼠。

碧：嗯。

海：用岩鹽把地鼠塗得厚厚的混在番薯石頭裡一起烤。（唱）好～香喲。

碧：那不衛生。

海：是嗎？姊姊妳以前都沒吃過嗎？

碧：（搖頭）有。

海：（笑唱）咖蘇咖蘇的烤地鼠，鹹鹹香脆；（說到）姊姊以前有吃過現在卻說不衛生？為什麼？

碧：（停下手上折紙，正色道。）妳該繼續練習了；（頓）正面腿抬得夠高了嗎？不要不方便長官進去，還有狗趴式呢？屁股翹夠高了？腰有下壓了？這樣才會比較緊。

海：噢。

（碧娜繼續折花。停頓。）

海：姊姊妳有吃過貓嗎？（碧娜聞未置理）莎夏姊姊呢？

碧：去找阿道夫長官看有沒有事幫忙。

海：怎麼有人這麼不喜歡休息時間呀？

碧：休息時間是留給有餘裕休息的人的。

海：什麼是餘裕呀？

碧：就是動作都練好、工作做好之後自己的時間。

海：那我就是不餘裕囉？（頓）可是莎夏姊已經把工作做得很好，為什麼還要去找阿道夫長官要工作呀？

碧：（停頓）我不知道。

海：噢，那我什麼時候可以有餘裕？

碧：等妳練好呀，責任制、責任制。

海：哼～嗯，那我就永遠都沒有餘裕啦；莎夏姐也不會有餘裕啦。

碧：為什麼？

海：阿道夫長官很忙，莎夏姊就有很多忙得幫；尤其莎夏姊最常幫的忙就是得一直繞著阿道夫長官。

碧：那才不叫幫忙。

海：噢；（突然想起）過貓好好吃噢！我只吃過一次，媽媽在面天溪旁摘

海倫娜

的；她說是偷偷摘的，因為要是被長老發現她到有天空的地方一定被
罵；脆脆又黏黏的好好吃，還有青草的香味。

碧：海倫娜。

（停頓）

海：姊姊，我想回家。

碧：回家。

海：回家？

碧：回家；我想吃好吃的白蝸牛。每年我生日媽媽都會烤迷迭蘚白蝸牛；
她會去東面窪谷刮迷迭蘚，褐褐綠綠的迷迭蘚，有一點點的汗臭味跟
辣辣嗆嗆的味道，是充滿香味的神奇粉末；再用地下濁溪旁潮濕的木
枝燒出白濃的煙霧，燻著QQ軟軟的白蝸牛肉，加上迷迭蘚香嗆微鹹
的口感跟煙薰的香味……。

海：不要說了。

碧：為、什、麼？我想回家，想媽媽。

碧：學會長大好嗎？海倫娜，不要像孩子一樣耍賴。

海：我本來就是。

碧：但妳現在不是了，現在妳不會有媽媽疼妳，她死了；所以也不會有人替妳煮生日的白蝸牛，懂嗎？

海：（哭起來）為什麼妳要這麼壞？我當然知道媽媽死了，因為她在我面前被打死的呀，我的媽媽她好可憐……。

碧：海倫娜。

海：海倫娜。

碧：海倫娜。

（海倫娜支支吾吾的不知道說什麼）

海：她眼睛瞪得大大看向我，眼睛裡面已經沒有星星，只有紅色的水一直流、一直流……。

碧：海倫娜，別說了。

海：怎麼可以不說，說的時候讓我可以想到，心情很好……或是心情很壞，然後我才會有感覺，覺得自己活著。

碧：但妳說了也於事無補，沒有用！無法解決的事說有什麼用、想有什麼
　　用？

海：我也不知道有什麼用……，說的時候會很生氣、很不甘願，再來就想
　　我可以怎麼做、要怎麼做？因為我不想要這樣繼續下去，不要。

碧：不可能。

海：不做怎麼知道不可能。

碧：乖，聽話好嗎？吃糖果嗎？（海倫娜搖頭）妳現在只要專心做好該做
　　的事，剩下的都不要管。

海：什麼是我該做的事？

碧：服務好長官們。

海：就算我不喜歡。

碧：（溫柔地）就算妳不喜歡。

海：其他的事呢？

碧：其他的事・目・前・都・不・重要。

海：這樣好像機器人。

碧：生活嘛。

海：我們都是機器人。

碧：這就是生活囉。

（海倫娜一邊唱著歌，一邊做著動作。）

（**歌曲**）〈酸酸歌〉

哼哼哼喲～

翹起來

壓下去

身體要會扭來扭去

嘴巴舔不會消失的棒棒糖

臭臭地（笑）

臭臭地

翻過來

抬起來

酸酸地

身體吃檸檬

酸酸的

眼睛也酸酸的

海：為什麼要工作？

碧：這是工作。

海：這是工作？

海：為什麼要工作？

碧：要換妳住的地方、妳穿的衣服，還有妳吃的食物。

海：就算我不喜歡。

碧：對，都是為了生活。

海：我寧願為了一顆糖果。

碧：糖果？（掏出一顆糖果）要嗎？

海：不是這種的，那種也算是…工作的；（笑）但不是為了生活。

碧：我不懂妳在說什麼？

海：以前在集中營（歌手開始唱起酸酸歌）有一個警衛叔叔，每過幾天就會來找我，每次給我一顆糖，晚上的時候，很晚；他說「妹妹，叔叔給妳糖果吃，要不要？」，糖果有好多種口味，甜甜的、酸酸的。

碧：（折著花）哇，叔叔對妳這麼好？在裡面還有糖果吃。

海：他都跟我玩遊戲，玩安靜遊戲，「糖果很好吃對不對？所以要慢慢含到全部都融化，不可以一下就咬碎；也不可以不小心吞下去或是掉出

來。」，叔叔會跟我玩問答遊戲，「妳叫什麼名字？」（搖頭），

「妳從哪裡來？」（搖頭），「妳的爸爸媽媽在哪裡？」（搖頭），

「妳最喜歡吃什麼？」我……（隨即搗上嘴巴，露出勝利的微笑）；

通過測試叔叔就會把棒棒放進來。像長官們一樣。

碧：妳怎麼允許他這麼做？

海：因為是遊戲呀。

碧：那是錯的。

海：他會慢慢地壓在我身上，一邊確認糖果沒有掉出來一邊輕輕地摸我，

在我耳邊說要乖乖、要乖乖，然後一點一點地把棒棒推進來。

碧：集中營裡不允許這樣的事，妳應該舉發他。

海：這不過是遊戲；叔叔總是說我做得很好，我也很喜歡，喜歡被稱讚、

喜歡吃糖果、喜歡叔叔溫柔地在我耳朵旁邊說話、喜歡叔叔像地下湖

的浪，一波波地輕輕推著我。

碧：（摀住海倫娜嘴巴）別說了。

海：又不能說。

碧：這是犯法的。

海：為什麼？長官們也對我做一樣的事，長官們就沒有犯法？

碧：人不一樣，長官不會犯法。

海：可是叔叔對我很好，每次想著遊戲就好像嚐到糖果甜甜香味；長官們只會讓我痛得一直哭，長官喜歡我哭，但我不喜歡哭。

碧：長官是長官，所以我們得做長官喜歡的，這是我們的工作；為了吃、住和穿。

海：我寧願只有一顆糖果。

碧：我寧願妳為了生活多努力；練習。

海：更多的練習、疼痛還有眼淚。

碧：親愛的海倫娜，沒有人喜歡眼淚，眼淚也不能幫助妳什麼；所以，別掉淚了；好好生活。

海：好好生活。

（海倫娜邊顫抖著、邊隱忍情緒的做著練習，碧娜折著花。）

間奏 石頭塔

（歌曲）〈石頭塔〉

石頭塔石頭塔

撿一顆石頭疊起來

把上面的破洞補起來

要小心　要小心

髒東西會掉下來

碰的一聲落下地

如果

還在喘　還在動

那就

讓石頭飛　把石頭砸

丟石頭不嫌累

聽到　停下來　停下來別理會

讓石頭一直飛　把石頭堆

直到只剩下石頭堆　哐哐響

丟石頭不嫌累

撿一顆石頭疊起來

石頭塔　石頭塔

（燈暗）

發現阿道夫

（十六歲的碧娜）

碧：在黑暗中的是誰。

（燈光變化，微暗的場上碧娜小心的警戒著。）

男：有誰在嗎？

碧：你⋯⋯是誰？

男：請幫幫我。

碧：你在哪裡？

男：妳再往前走就會看到我了，幫幫我。

碧：你在哪裡？

男：我在這裡。

碧：你在哪裡？

男：再往前走。

碧：你在哪裡？我沒有看到你。

男：在黑暗中，妳仔細看。

（燈光越加昏暗，男人的話語聲不斷重複且空洞感越來越強。）

碧：我找不到你。

男：妳再往黑暗裡走一點，有沒有看到我，我在黑暗中不是這麼容易看到的，就像災厄一樣，災厄不會在白天出現，只會隱身在黑暗中伺機攻擊；那就是我，妳有發現嗎？請幫幫我，我斷了腿走不動。

碧：我已經在黑暗中了，但是我還是找不到你。

男：在更裡面一點的地方，在黑暗的核心；一個妳潛意識裡避免碰觸的地方，有看到嗎？

碧：我找不到你，你有辦法聽著我的聲音往我這靠近嗎？

男：災禍本身不會主動向人靠近，不過如果妳期待、呼告，那麼它就會出現。

阿：我的腿斷了，沒有辦法動了。

碧：發出一些聲響，讓我知道你在哪？

（傳出一些帶有不詳感覺的重複聲響）

男：妳知道災厄會招來毀滅，為什麼還要在黑暗中尋找它呢？放任它的消亡、放任它的消亡、放任它的消亡、放任它的消亡……。（此句與前面的聲音交互疊合。）

（歌曲）〈壞壞的黑暗〉

黑暗是壞壞的

呀喔～呀喲～壞壞的

摸不清的快樂

還是魅惑的神祕

壞壞的黑暗
盡情的擺爛
我要踏進黑暗裡
享受壞壞的黑暗
崩壞的刺激
媽媽說別對黑暗使力
因為妳無法駕馭
可是呀喲喲　我愛壞壞的黑暗
探險的快感

（音樂結束，回到一片靜默之中）

碧：不用擔心，我快找到你了，你怎麼會受傷的。

阿：我摔進一個洞穴裡，求救了老半天卻沒有人來救我；所以我試著爬出

去，卻發現另個一個通道，於是我沿著通道不斷地往前爬……；妳快

碧：你繼續說，就快找到你了。

找到我了嗎？

阿：原本只能爬行的通道到後來越來越高，好像是有人修築過的；一開始
我以為這是某個廢棄的礦坑，後來我想……這會不會是傳說中的地下
人世界。

阿：妳找到我了嗎？

碧：我看到你了。

阿：看來我獲救了，（碧娜抬起一顆石頭）沒想到地底真的有人！我發現
地下世界、發現地底人了！這個發現一定會震驚世界。

碧：你怎麼不動。

阿：我的腿好像斷了、動不了，妳會扶我去你們的村落治療對嗎？我看不
到妳在哪裡，這裡好冷，我好痛又好不舒服。

碧：你是誰？

（碧娜高舉石頭。燈光變化。）

阿：我是胥納的阿道夫。

（燈暗。一段音樂，如同碧娜心中波濤洶湧的混亂，面對是否殺死阿道夫與母親沉痛提醒在腦中拉鋸，一種新生活的綺想與舊日陳腔濫調交互疊合的混亂。演員在黑暗中如同剪影般停止在碧娜高舉石頭，並以極慢的速度放下石頭。）

阿：妳當時為什麼不丟石頭？

碧：我不知道。

阿：就算妳帶我回去，難道其他人不會在我身上疊起石頭塔嗎？

碧：有人的確想，也有人不想。所以我問長老，我們的不可爭執、不可離間和不可憤怒呢？為什麼大家為了一個地上人可以分裂、仇視。

阿：然後。

碧：然後你就被放出來了。

阿：如果同樣的問題妳會怎麼回答？

碧：（不置可否的聳肩）我根本不知道，也不是想證實什麼，只是單純覺得「我不想決定並且殺掉我眼前這個人。」，但我也不能隨便的把你丟著不管，畢竟這不是可以隨便置之不理的問題。

（停頓；阿道夫意味深長地看著碧娜，碧娜別過頭；突然地變化。）

碧：這裡是我的神祕小洞，從來沒有人來過。

阿：為什麼讓我看？

碧：你喜歡嗎？

阿：很原始、充滿生機。

碧：只要心情不好的時候，我就會到我的小洞宣洩情緒，這裡是我的出口；明明只是一個小洞，真是神奇；你覺得呢？

阿：我想它絕對是很棒的，只是我無法體會。

碧：我喜歡這種濕潤、溫熱的感覺，我好渴，你渴嗎？

阿：我還好。

碧：（拿出水瓶試圖打開栓子）我好渴噢，嗯～嗯～啊。我不行。

阿：我試試看。（接過瓶子後試圖打開栓子）喔，我沒辦法。還是不行就算了。

碧：我試試（拿回罐子），喔……好緊……好緊。

阿：還是很緊嗎？

碧：沒關係，好緊

碧：真的可以嗎？

碧：再試試可以嗎？

阿：那快出來了嗎？

碧：……好像有鬆一點點了。

碧：鬆了、鬆了，（將瓶子遞給阿道夫）你感覺到了嗎？

阿：好像真的沒那麼緊了。

碧：那我繼續囉。

阿：嗯。

碧：啊！啊！啊！快出來了！快出來了！（栓子被拔出）喔！出來了。

阿：終於出來了。妳很累吧？

碧：還好。

阿：（頓）如果那時候我身上被堆了石頭塔，妳要怎麼辦？

碧：（搖晃水瓶）那我現在會渴得不得了。（碧娜喝水）

阿：我沒幫上妳什麼忙，像個殘廢一樣。

碧：你陪在我旁邊就夠了。

阿：是嗎？（停頓）還記得我教你捲的花嗎？

碧：嗯。

阿：那是我最喜歡的花，叫玫瑰；玫瑰有很多種顏色，但我覺得真正的玫瑰必定要是紅色的；它們的莖帶有刺人的棘，於是它們嬌豔的像是在引誘人卻又張狂地用棘拒絕人。

碧：你是玫瑰嗎？

阿：（搖頭）我只是阿道夫。（頓）我就要回去了，或許有一天我會回來
　　地下，會帶一朵玫瑰來看妳。

碧：在此之前我就不停地捲著玫瑰花等你。

（靜默）

阿：當初為什麼救我？

碧：我沒有救你，我說過的，我只是單純不想做決定。

阿：但妳把我帶回去給眾人決定我的死活，也是一種決定不是嗎？（碧
　　娜愕然）妳後悔了嗎？

碧：我想大家。

（燈暗）

間奏 老鼠

（兩個戴著老鼠面具的人站在舞台上，靜止。）

（音樂：垃圾山；複雜、不規律、不協調和各種突兀的，好似是對生命的謳歌，用的卻是穢物、屍體和難以入耳的辱罵；有繽紛色彩堆高的垃圾高聳巨大，隨時發生小型滑落；細看亦可發現多處簡陋但得以窩身的空間。

場景：這是世界的堆肥處，人小小的走在裡面，小小像蛆般的鑽窟，也製造幾處硝煙直插天際，早已無法辨識原色的灰黑烏鳥順著煙柱盤旋。相較於沉默探挖的成年人，有翹著尾巴的瘦狗跟著稱之為孩子的小人奔跑，但他們絕不是我們想的，單純。）

（音樂強烈霸佔空間，兩位演員呼吸逐漸加重，細看才發現 Ａ 是帶有興奮的情緒，B則是逐漸困難；就在B困難地要倒下時迅速挺直，A則迅速如動物般四肢在地奔跑，而後注意到B靜止站立，也跟著站立，並數度調整姿態直到與B相仿。靜默，A有時不耐騷動，又隨即恢復，並在幾次音樂影響下瘋狂扭動，B則是有禮但逐漸顯露不耐，最後走向麥克風。）

B：沒⋯⋯。

A：（模仿B）沒有。

B：沒有音樂。

（音樂結束）

A：音樂不好嗎？

B：沒有。

A：嗯。（音樂隨即如同無法按捺的響起）

B：但是⋯⋯沒有音樂。

（音樂結束）

A：為什麼？

B：首先，我尊重你對音樂的享受以及聽的權利，並且我也不會對你所聽的嘈雜、刺耳、令人心浮氣躁的垃圾音樂提出任何批評，其實我也不介意繼續聽下去，但不是現在。

A：那是什麼時候。

B：時間到了你就會知道。

A：欸，妳喜歡嗎？

B：喜歡什麼？

A：我。

B：你?!你好髒，全身充滿細菌。

A：是嗎？

B：還有你猥瑣的樣子。

A：欸？

B：你怎麼可以這麼自甘墮落？

（A開始玩起「自甘墮落」）

A：妳不喜歡我們聽的音樂？

B：不喜歡。

A：沒有什麼讓妳喜歡的？

B：拜託，當然沒有。

A：為什麼？

B：你是一隻老鼠。

A：妳也是啊。

B：我拒絕承認我是一隻猥瑣、骯髒並且粗俗的髒老鼠。

A：為什麼？

B：因為我受過教育。

A：教育會改變妳是一隻老鼠的事實嗎？

B：教育會改變我的視野。

A：看不起其他的老鼠嗎？

B：我沒有說。

A：但妳表現出來了。

B：我尊重你，但不代表我得了解你。

A：那尊重不就顯得虛假。

B：我才是有受教育的老鼠好嗎？憑什麼你說話來一副很有知識的樣子？

A：我不知道。

B：很好；現在請帶著你的音樂還有你們骯髒和粗俗的生活離開這裡。

A：留妳一個人？

B：對，留我一個人。

A：這樣妳不孤單嗎？

B：我得在一個優雅、整潔的環境才能生活。

A：那其他老鼠呢？

B：變得像我一樣或被淘汰，只有和我具備同樣高度的才配跟我生活、對話。

A：妳有尖尖的鼻子。

B：是。

A：還有兩顆大門牙。

B：嗯哼。

A：但妳的教育出了什麼問題？

B：什麼？

A：它讓你忘了自己是誰；碧娜。

（燈暗）

莎夏

（碧娜一邊折著花、一邊看著莎夏和海倫娜的遺骸。）

碧：如果妳們還活著，妳們會跟我說什麼？像是「今天去野溪捕白魚。」

或是「為海倫娜煮幾顆白蝸牛吧……。」這樣的話嗎？我現在一個人吃得好隨便，海倫娜，妳最愛的白蝸牛現在到處都有，不會有人跟妳搶了，不用等到妳生日才能吃噢，姊姊隨時都能烤給妳吃；妳媽媽以前採迷迭蘚是用刮刀在岩壁上輕輕地摳才能刮下一些粉末對吧？姊姊可以大手筆地鋪上一層厚厚的迷迭蘚，沒有人在摘了。什麼？白魚嗎？（笑）我已經很久沒吃白魚了，一年多前我還在野溪那邊看到地上人的攝影隊，說是找尋最後的地下人，我不想太高調，做好自己份內的事；所以我也就很少過去了，免得又遇到他們；但我想莎夏妳要是看到了，一定衝上前去……，對不對？

莎：對不對什麼？（碧娜呆愣了一下，無法意識到莎夏真的回話。莎夏一邊笑一邊端著一盤水果走出來。）妳幹嘛呀？

碧：（吞吞吐吐的）妳去哪裡了？

莎：我去阿道夫先生那裡幫忙了呀，不然我還能去哪裡。

碧：妳怎麼讓我等了這麼久。

莎：妳發什麼神經呀。海倫娜呢？

碧：我不知道。

莎：妳不知道？不是說要幫忙盯著她嗎？老是不學好整天閒晃，表現不好會給阿道夫先生添麻煩的。

碧：是嗎？

莎：怎麼不是？妳可以不要整天只顧著捲妳手上的花嗎？快去找海倫娜啊；我休息一下。跟在阿道夫先生身邊太累了，整天頂著一張撲克臉，問他問題也不回，幫他做好事情也不會表示謝意，我都快受不了了，更何況其他人。（頓）還在看什麼，去找海倫娜啊。

碧：我回來妳還會在嗎？

莎：妳說什麼廢話，當然不在。

碧：妳要去哪？

莎：小姐，妳是陪長官high陪到ㄎ一ㄤ掉了嗎？我除了去找阿道夫先生外還能去哪。

碧：一定要去嗎？

莎：廢話，他沒有我事情做得完嗎？

碧：妳可以陪我嗎？

莎：神經病，陪妳幹嘛？

碧：陪我決定一些事情。

莎：碧娜，我沒有興趣陪你決定事情，自己決定不就好了；反正你工作之餘除了折花也沒別的事了不是嗎？別拿這種事煩我好嗎？

碧：阿道夫就這麼重要嗎？

莎：（頓住）阿道夫、阿道夫，妳不會加個先生嗎？我不管妳以前跟他有多好，記得自己現在的身分。

碧：那妳這樣一直纏著他又是為什麼？

莎：為什麼？難不成要像妳整天窩在這邊折花？還是憑著跟阿道夫先生的舊交情過日子，別當吸血蟲好嗎？

碧：做自己份內的事，莎夏，我們的責任是服侍好長官們，妳這樣整天往阿道夫先生那裡跑，不怕他生氣？

莎：阿道夫先生有我高興都來不及了，（頓）碧娜，要是妳不服氣大可一起來呀。

碧：莎夏。

莎：幹嘛？

碧：妳不覺得這樣太招搖了嗎？

莎：招搖？怎麼樣招搖？

碧：整天膩在阿道夫先生身旁。

莎：妳嫉妒嗎？

碧：妳再說什麼？

莎：（用手托著自己的胸部再壓住下部）妳覺得靠這些可以撐多久？是啦，我們對外就是上節目、上通告，成為接受地上社會教育的優良地下人；但事實上，我們只是長官們的玩具，這點應該不用我提醒妳吧？

碧：不用。

莎：那妳覺得長官會對我們感興趣到什麼時候？還是妳覺得電視、廣播通告會一直一直下去？這社會遲早會對我們失去興趣，到時候妳還剩什麼？去節目上講著達達、野獸、田園、抽象的美學屁話嗎？還是妳要回去早就已經被摧毀殆盡的地下？（情緒激動的）由阿道夫先生（手莎：（突然失去元氣般的）高層不就決定送我們回來了嗎？

（燈光變化成一種萎靡、虛弱的感覺）

碧：如果妳不發動遊行抗爭，會不會現在我們還可以待在地上。

莎：幹嘛？

碧：莎夏。

莎：（將手上的花以拋物線的方式丟開）。

那種。（離開碧娜後突然回頭）還有，阿道夫先生有一天會對我笑的

我想要妳幫我佈置一整面牆的花，像顏料噴灑四散，細細小小蔓延的

到時候要我養妳和海倫娜也是可以啦。（抽走碧娜手上的花）到時候

長官、沒有目光放在我們身上，我也可以活下去。（拍拍碧娜的臉）

莎：過去的事說再多都沒有用了，我要努力在地上社會活著，有一天沒有

（莎夏停頓，稍稍整理情緒。）

指著碧娜）一手主導的地下毀滅政策。

碧：可是或許他們看我們乖乖的就又會心軟了。

莎：妳覺得他們有這麼好心嗎？

碧：你把遊行抗爭搞得太大了。

莎：我是為了讓我們三個在地上活著，最後三個地下人。

碧：我知道。

莎：在阿道夫先生自殺之後我們只能靠自己。對我們最好的阿道夫先生背負著所有罵名和罪過自殺了。（冷笑）說什麼「讓地下人回到他們的世界」，我們早就一無所有了。

碧：從被送到地上社會開始，一直到被遣返，妳都這麼積極。

莎：妳想說什麼？

碧：身為地下人遺族，妳會不會太強勢？

莎：我爭取有錯嗎？我為了自己有錯嗎？我的家被搗爛了，親人被殺光了，為什麼還殘忍的要我回來面對一切？我想留在地上社會就是錯的？就是冷血、不愛故鄉？

（莎夏開始劇烈咳嗽）

碧：莎夏，妳還好嗎？

莎：我要走了。

碧：妳要去哪裡？

莎：我感覺到我的最後三日已經要來了。

碧：別走。

莎：我必須要走了。

碧：我求求妳，別留下我跟海倫娜。

莎：我們又回到大地母神的肚腹裡，我幫妳們先去看看新世界長什麼樣子。

碧：妳會在最後三日改變妳曾經做過的決定嗎？

莎：不會，一個都不會。

（莎夏說完後，整個人癱軟在地；碧娜瘋狂地搖晃莎夏。）

碧：莎夏！莎夏！不要走！不要做任何決定就不會有最後三日！不要！不要！莎夏！我的最後三日呢？莎夏！

（男子睜開眼，伸手清脆的打了碧娜一巴掌。）

男：我是阿道夫。

（燈暗）

間奏 雞與牛

（段落開始時場上呈現單一，卻以一種極慢的狀態進行侵蝕，直到最後原本的單一轉而被另一種強烈而富有侵略性的狀態取代。）

雞：歸歸歸，不歸。

牛：哞～喔。

雞：歸歸歸，不歸。

牛：哞～～喔。

（牛反芻咀嚼）

雞：卜歸……歸歸歸，不歸。

（牛反芻咀嚼）

雞：呱呱呱。（來回走動）歸歸歸，不歸。

（牛反芻咀嚼）

雞：歸歸歸。

（牛反芻咀嚼，雞來回走動）

牛：雞，你在找什麼？

雞：找死。

牛：哞～（繼續反芻）

雞：牛，你在等什麼？

牛：等死。

雞：不歸、不歸；牛有幾種死法？

牛：（不解地）嗯？

雞：我們有幾千幾萬隻雞，但只有一種死法。

牛：了解哞～～～。

（雞脖子伸長、雙腳亂踢，接著發出帶有咕魯和逐漸失去的雞鳴聲，接著像被丟入溫熱水中浮沉，再被拎起丟入脫毛滾筒，雞一邊旋轉一邊自己發

出肉身撞擊滾筒控咚控咚的聲響；重複數次。牛一邊咀嚼一邊觀看。雞作

嘔。）

牛：暈啦。

雞：其實不會，一隻雞一生轉一次。不不不歸～。

（雞做出套索的動作繞在牛身上）

牛：換我啦，哞。

（雞帶著牛繞行至定點，將手上的綁繩綁在地上並且從遠方拿來巨大、沉重的榔頭，牛發出哞哞的鳴叫但並不走動的原地踱步；雞計算落下的軌跡，來回筆劃幾次，牛定定地看著雞，雞將手上的榔頭重擊在牛頭上，牛應聲倒地，搖晃著頭擺動四肢，雞上前去用刀劃開牛的脖子，牛發出哞哞的嘶聲，雞坐到旁邊看著。）

雞：歸歸歸～不歸，歸歸歸～不歸；（停頓）妳為什麼不逃，碧娜。

通報

（碧娜捲著手上的花，好像聽到什麼似的停下手上的動作，確認沒有聲響後繼續捲花；突然地暫停手上動作並彈跳起來；巨大的聲響和閃光突然從遠方不斷傳來，通過岩層傳遞震動；有些許的聲響、人聲搭配來回衝擊的回音，形成某種奇異的旋律，彷若哀嚎又像和聲、吟詠；殺戮正在遠方形成。碧娜嘴裡念著「石頭塔」。）

阿：碧娜。

（碧娜停止念「石頭塔」，在強大的音樂和燈光下凝止，或說以奇特的表情看著阿道夫，而後以極瘋狂的方式吼叫出「阿道夫」三個字，音樂和燈光也像退潮般的迅速退至遠方。）

碧：阿道夫；（給阿道夫看手上的花）你看，我在捲花。

阿：碧娜……。

碧：你看我折了這麼多花，從你離開之後我想著我們到花谷看花，想著你說的玫瑰花，你教的，我一朵一朵地捲，每個人都歡喜地問我這美麗的花叫什麼名字，每個人都說「碧娜，下一朵是給我的噢。」，大家給我紙、給我布，讓我做出玫瑰花，大家都比較著哪朵玫瑰花美，有好幾個女孩想跟我學做玫瑰花，她們的媽媽說「這是碧娜的玫瑰花，別去煩她，等她捲給我們，好嗎」？；其實我可以教她們捲。

阿：碧娜，夏楠區侵略開始了！現在逃還得及，回去跟長老說，快帶著大家逃。

碧：然後、然後從伊色諜區被地上世界發現，侵略開始；逃往北方的人說是由一個地上世界的人主導、帶著軍隊……。

阿：碧娜，我知道妳有很多事情想說，但現在不是敘舊的時候。

碧：有人被殺了、屍體疊成山高，有人被帶走……聽說被抓去當苦工……。

阿：碧娜，我知道軍隊會怎麼對你們，所以快逃好嗎？

碧：原本插在頭上、別在胸口、掛在門旁一朵朵玫瑰花都被摘掉、丟在地上，我手邊沒有等著要被捲的材料了；大家都知道那位主導侵略地下世界的人是「阿道夫」。

阿：阿道夫。

碧：阿道夫。

阿：阿道夫。

碧：阿道夫。

阿：阿道夫。

碧：阿道夫。

阿：阿道夫。

碧：阿道夫。

阿：阿道夫。

碧：阿道夫。

阿：阿道夫。

碧：阿道夫。（兩人大笑起來）阿道夫，你讓我等了好久；你看我捲的玫瑰花像不像？

阿：像。

碧：我一直在捲玫瑰花；那天在花谷裡你說下次碰面你會帶一朵真正的玫瑰花給我，你帶了嗎？

阿：對不起，碧娜。

碧：你忘記了呀？那好吧；（搗住自己的臉後又打開）阿道夫，這次你帶了嗎？（阿道夫搖頭，碧娜再次搗住臉後又打開。）阿道夫，你帶了嗎？

阿：沒有；碧娜，現在不是說這個的時候。

碧：我記得那天在花谷裡，你說玫瑰花有多美麗，你說下次我們碰面你要從地上為我帶一朵的；我等了好多年。

阿：我回到地上之後，又經歷了很多事；（停頓）但現在不是說這個的時候，快去跟長老說，帶著全族人往北逃吧。

碧：（搖頭）你何不自己去說，我只等一朵玫瑰花，而不是一個消息。

阿：碧娜，妳怎麼了？現在可是攸關生死的事。

碧：那你何不自己去。

阿：我沒辦法離開營區太久，貿然進到妳們村落會引起不必要的爭執和拖延。

碧：我曾經帶著你回去，現在我也可以帶著你回去。

阿：碧娜，我得走了。

碧：你必須要自己去告訴他們這個消息，就像當初我帶你回去讓他們決定你的死活一樣。

阿：為什麼不能請妳代為傳達呢？我們時間有限呀。

碧：因為我只負責把人帶到他們面前，而不是宣告一個消息，上次是，這次也會是。

阿：地上社會為了發展地下礦產和能源，發布了許多命令，已經展開全面屠殺、侵占，我們的時間真的不多了。

碧：我們這裡沒有任何資源，難道不能進行任何溝通嗎？你們文明進步的地上社會。

阿：不能。

碧：帶我去找你們的負責人呢？說不定我能帶著長老的信去求和。

阿：沒辦法，因為目前策略就是全面淨空地下、進行資源探勘。

碧：別跟我說不可能，帶我去找這個策略的最高負責人，不試試怎麼知道？

阿：不用找了。

碧：為什麼？

阿：因為就在你面前。

碧：我面前只有你呀，一個只負責帶玫瑰花的傢伙。

阿：碧娜，回去地上之後我被關進精神病院幾年，他們說這個國家沒有地下世界，所有人都不相信我，後來政府高層相信我，把我從精神病院救出來，器重我；你了解我的難處嗎？

碧：我不會代替你去傳達什麼的，要去你自己去。

阿：碧娜，別為難我；你們曾經對我這麼好。

碧：那就給我一朵玫瑰花。

阿：別提什麼該死的玫瑰花！

碧：我等的也不是屠殺！（停頓）我們再重來一次；阿道夫，好多年不見！你終於要帶玫瑰花給我了嗎？（阿道夫搖頭）快說是啊，你帶了玫瑰花給我；我只要玫瑰花，其他的我都不要。

阿：可惜我帶的不是玫瑰花。

碧：別的我都不要，不要口信、消息；「她是讓地下世界被發現的碧娜！」、「是她讓地上世界的人活在我們的國度！」、「南區淪陷了，什麼時候會輪到我們？都是碧娜害的！」，不可離間啊大家，不可憤怒呀大家，不可爭執呀大家，所以大家把我捲好的玫瑰花剪碎、丟在地上，所以大家當作我不存在。你走了，就這麼輕易地走了，卻沒有想過留下來的人有多痛苦！我每天每天都要承受這樣的痛苦！

（停頓）所以，我只要一朵玫瑰花。

阿：我很抱歉，碧娜；我真的沒辦法再待下去了，拜託妳去跟大家說，快逃吧！對不起。

（阿道夫停下來）

碧：我最喜歡的玫瑰花。

（阿道夫欲離開）

阿：我很抱歉，碧娜；我真的沒辦法再待下去了，拜託妳去跟大家說，快逃吧！對不起。

（阿道夫欲離開）

阿：像鮮血。

碧：還有它的荊棘。

阿：像枯骨。對不起。

（阿道夫離開）

碧：我不會去傳達任何事的，我只等著那朵玫瑰花。

（轟炸和殺戮的燈光、音樂像是海嘯般湧至，碧娜站著不動。突然靜
默。）

（歌曲）〈花未開〉

　我　最愛的　玫瑰花

　還沒開

（燈暗）

凍死

阿：春天。

碧：岩壁上的綠色青苔開始萌發，陽光照射的谷地呈現草木扶疏的景象；對了，還有鳥也會飛進來築巢，媽媽說谷地危險、容易被看到，其實還是有很多人偷偷跑去玩。

阿：還有花。

碧：花，我們的花像是用各種顏料噴灑四散的小點，細細小小的蔓延在整個洞穴內。

阿：和地上不同。

碧：（搭上阿道夫）和地上不同，你說地上有巴掌大的蓮花，像奏鳴的喇叭一般的百合花，顏色衝突的三色堇；各種花卉爭奇鬥豔，各自驕傲奔放的展示、渲染整片大地，……還有我最喜歡的玫瑰花。

阿：春天。

碧：春天。岩壁上的綠色青苔開始萌發，被陽光照射的谷地呈現草木扶疏的景象；對了，還有鳥也會飛進來築巢，媽媽說谷地危險、容易被看到，其實還是有很多人偷偷跑去玩。

阿：還有花。

碧：我最喜歡的玫瑰花。

阿：你們的花像是用各種顏料噴灑四散的小點，細細小小的蔓延在整個洞穴內。

碧：和地上不同。

阿：還有妳最喜歡的玫瑰花。

碧：鮮紅的布滿整個花園。

阿：像鮮血。

碧：還有它們的荊棘。

阿：像枯骨。

碧：我最喜歡的……春天；岩壁上的綠色青苔開始萌發，陽光照射的谷地呈現草木扶疏的景象；；對了，還有鳥也會飛進來築巢，媽媽說谷地危險、容易被看到，其實還是有很多人偷偷跑去玩。

阿：偷偷跑去玩。

碧：偷偷跑去玩，草地就像大地的綠色絨毯，不是黃褐尖銳凹凸的石礫地；連我們長滿後繭的腳都能感覺來自腳底的柔軟。

阿：都能感覺來自腳底的柔軟。

碧：來自腳底的柔軟，還有用葉片進行的遊戲。

阿：用葉子折出小船。

碧：用葉子折出湯匙。

阿：用葉子吹出哨音。

碧：噓!!（笑）媽媽說谷地危險、容易被看到，這樣會被聽到。

阿：還是有很多人偷偷跑去玩。

碧：我最喜歡的……春天；岩壁上的綠色青苔開始萌發，陽光照射的谷地呈現草木扶疏的景象。

阿：還有妳最喜歡的玫瑰花。

碧：鮮紅的布滿整個花園。

阿：像鮮血。

碧：還有它們的荊棘。

阿：像枯骨。

碧：還有我喜歡的玫瑰花。

（歌曲）〈春天〉

　　春天

　　噢

凍死

097

偷偷跑去玩的　春天

視網膜都是綠色的

春天

熱烈生長

充滿喜樂

的

春天

阿：跟洞穴深處傳來腐臭的氣味。

（音樂、燈光變化）

阿：洞穴深處傳來腐臭的氣味。

（碧娜仿若無聞）

阿：腐臭的氣味。

（停頓）

阿：腐臭的。

（靜默）

阿：腐臭。妳曾經說過那個故事。

碧：（停頓）那不是故事。

阿：但讓我印象深刻，早春時四處飄散的腐臭腥味。

碧：（微笑地）地下世界到了夏天是難以忍受的炎熱，為了避開燠熱的暑氣，於是人們帶著輕便的行囊沿著天然的地洞往下爬，逐漸擁擠也讓陰涼的地洞變熱，人們不斷往下、更往下，為了享受涼爽舒適的溫度。如此讓人忘了上頭酷熱的夏天；轉眼就到秋天，有些人離開、有些人依然留戀地洞深處的舒適溫度；我們總是會把食物準備得很充足。

阿：但秋冬交際總會在某一日氣溫驟降，無法預知地從極北吹來冷冽的強

凍死

099

風。來不及往上爬的人就會在很短的時間內冷死，並且被凍住，等到來年春天解凍、腐爛，於是整個春天便瀰漫著腐臭的氣味。

碧：還有各色點綴洞穴的小花盛開。枯骨無法阻止往下爬的決心，人們踩過骨骸往更涼爽的地方去。

阿：要熬過一個炎熱的夏天不如往舒服的地方去，就算來不及在北風刮起前離開不過幾秒內便被凍死，妳是這樣跟我說的。

碧：大部分的人都是這樣說。

阿：那妳呢？

碧：我還記得在某個秋冬來臨之際，在地洞深處；遠方的阿姑婆突然喊著。

阿：北風來啦。

碧：阿姑婆本來精神就不太正常，幸好她女兒十分孝順，每到夏天就帶著她往地洞下來；但她吵吵鬧鬧的把大家都搞得精神緊張。

姑：北風來了。

碧：阿姑婆，沒有北風。

姑：北風來了。

碧：阿姑姨呢？怎麼讓妳一個人在外面跑，回去妳的洞。

姑：北風來啦，蘚妹被凍住了、蘚妹被凍住了。

碧：喔，我知道了，阿姑姨在睡覺妳偷跑出來。

姑：快逃呀，北風吹來了。幼妹，妳快逃。

碧：阿姑婆，我帶妳回去往阿姑姨。

（碧娜帶阿姑姨走，被帶往反方向。）

姑：春巧呢？

碧：媽媽她往上面一點點去買東西了。

姑：快逃！我們去找妳媽媽。

碧：阿姑婆，妳先等一下啦，妳看大家都開始緊張了；（對四周）沒事、

凍死

101

沒事，她有點精神不正常。

（一股銳利而猛烈的隆隆聲由遠至近）

姑：（將碧娜往前推倒）快逃啦！（阿姑婆隨即冰凍）

碧：我才知道原來北風像一堵白牆，一撞上人就硬住了。一瞬間，有的人因為探頭出來看我跟阿姑婆的動靜，就一顆頭被凍住……然後腳一軟頭像西瓜摔爛在地上。我逃，心慌地往上跑，看到我媽就一把抓住她往上爬，直到穿到安全層；有一群和我們一樣倉皇逃竄的人，我們看著帶著冰霜的北風就在下面掃來掃去，把來不及爬上來的人凍在爬梯上、凝結在路上，原本一陣一陣的北風越來越強直到整個地洞變成白色一片，寒氣透上來，我們一邊打著哆嗦一邊掉眼淚，有人哭天搶地、不停哀嚎，聲聲呼喚著，直到暈了被扛走，也有人不發一語地坐在旁邊，也有少數幾個在大家來不及反應時跳進地洞，……下一刻傳來的通常是像玻璃碎掉的聲音。（停頓）接著我們各自回家，用一整

地下女子

102

個冬天替亡者們哀悼。

阿：妳有因此對地洞恐懼。

碧：（搖頭）隔年夏天，我和家人回到地洞避暑。

阿：隔年春天，阿姑婆變成腐臭的氣味。

（碧娜不置可否地聳肩，燈暗。）

間奏　胎動

（碧娜蜷曲著躺在血泊之中，男人坐在池畔輕輕地用腳踢水、蕩起漣漪；

許久，碧娜微微擺動手肘、伸展四肢直到自己坐起身；碧娜坐在血泊中，

男人坐在池畔輕輕地用腳踢水、蕩起漣漪；許久，碧娜新奇而緩慢地對四

周張望並站起來，男人坐在池畔輕輕地用腳踢水、蕩起漣漪；許久，碧娜

以充滿感激和莊嚴的神情往前走至池畔前緣。男人坐在池畔輕輕地用腳踢

水。）

男：碧娜，妳‧還‧在‧這喔，沒有移動‧到‧哪裡去。

（停頓，燈暗。）

地下女子

104

在集中營

（男人默默地換了一身衣裝，回到碧娜身旁，碧娜呆坐著，雙眼直視前方。）

莎：他叫拉轟。

碧：誰？

莎：剛剛被拖走的那一個。

碧：嗯。

莎：他的女兒這幾天拉肚子拉得很嚴重。

碧：誰的女兒？

莎：拉轟的女兒；他替孩子去醫務室偷藥被發現了。

碧：嗯。

莎：他會被砍斷手腳後放進水池裡，活活淹死。

碧：是嗎？

莎：19床的羅輝、23床的財元、36床秀蘚、41床春草、44床美光、53床水美昨晚睡了就沒再起床了。

碧：（微微側頭）妳都知道呀。

莎：6床的石仲夥同83床的長溪挖了一條逃跑的密道也被發現了。

碧：我有聽說。

莎：（微微挑眉）聽說？（無事地）從前天開始他們就被吊在廣場上，用鐵鉤穿過肩胛骨的吊在那邊，活活地。直到他們斷氣前都一直咒罵著地上社會的殘暴；妳有經過廣場吧？大家繼續視而不見地上工，為什麼呀？

碧：因為我們被教育不可離間。

莎：是呀。

（靜默）

莎：昨天，C區的人偷偷摸摸想搬走我們的食物，被57床的楊花看到，她嚷嚷著大家快來抓賊，92床的石晶也氣得和楊花一起罵C區的人；但不知道為什麼C區的人膽子這麼大，搬著我們的配給直直往C營區走，楊花氣不過、上前拉住他們，跟著吆喝大家來幫忙評評理；妳知道這件事嗎？

碧：我在那裡。

莎：C區的人諾諾地說「我們沒偷、我們沒偷」一邊擺開楊花的手，C區的人雖然動作不大但人終究比較多，光靠她們兩個人怎麼可能擋得住，石晶氣死了，她對大家吼，「我們飯已經不夠吃了！妳們為什麼還放任他們明目張膽的搬走我們明天的飯？」，沒有人說話，楊花扯著嗓門吼「大家快來幫忙呀！自己的飯菜自己救！自己的飯菜自己救！」（停頓）看到原本安靜圍觀的人有點騷動了，石晶趕緊抱著菜桶喊「快來幫忙」，幾個人也吼著上前幫忙，雖然C區人多，但有人阻擋他們當然無法順利抬走飯菜桶，慌亂之中有人打翻了半桶菜。（頓）然後碰、碰、碰的幾聲槍響，石晶、楊花和幾個幫忙的人全被打死了，C區的人聽到槍響就靜靜地趴在地上，所以沒一個人吃到子彈，然後他們又靜靜地從地上爬起來，靜靜地抬起飯、菜桶，靜靜地離開。我衝到現場的時候她們倒在地上，人群還在……可是沒有人上前替他們闔上眼睛，我聽到有人說「由他們搬嘛，何必賠上一條命？」，有人說「都是因為他們這麼吵，怎麼不先找管理員報備呢？」，也有人說「不可爭執呀，你看這是不是報應」，……還有人說「浪費了半鍋飯菜。」。（看著碧娜，碧娜發現自己一直被盯著。）

碧：（慌張地摸自己的臉）怎麼了嗎？

（莎夏搖搖頭。）

莎：我一邊咬著牙，眼淚不停不停地滴，上前去幫石晶她們睜著老大的眼晴闊上，我好生氣、好生氣，所以我站在她們的血泊之中瞪著圍觀的人，狠狠地、像是要在他們臉上揍地瞪著他們，大家都嚇到了，有人往後退了幾步、有人不知道該怎麼辦，然後我聽到人群中有人小小聲地說……。

碧：不可憤怒。

莎：對，不可憤怒；原本是一個小小的聲音，然後第二個人說、第三個，大家開始以同樣的音量、節奏和緩地對著我說「不可憤怒、不可憤怒、不可憤怒……。」，好像憤怒是我的錯。（頓）管理員來了，帶著工班的人把屍體一具具撿走，人群散了，剩我一個站在那裡。

莎：妳覺得呢？

碧：（搖頭）我覺得很難過。

莎：（笑）我也很難過，那群人裡或許也有人很難過，但是他們還是散開了，還是去忙各自的事情；連血都被鋪上一層土灰，什麼都不剩。

在集中營
109

碧：我知道。

（莎夏搖頭。燈光變化。歌手演唱〈你不知道〉。）

（歌曲）〈你不知道〉

飢餓的煎熬

飽足的美妙

你怎麼會不知道

死亡，你知道

毀滅，你知道

你用嘴朗讀好多遍

你用眼睛閱覽好多遍

但你從來都沒有親身體驗

家園若不在你面前破落傾倒

那痛你怎麼會知道

自己沒有真的傷痛

你會願意知道

眼淚一直掉　一直掉

轉身繼續無視微笑

你真的知道？

那下一步要怎麼走

你知不知道？

你知不知道

你知

不
知
道

（燈光變化）

莎：妳知道我是誰嗎？

碧：我不知道；對不起。

莎：沒關係。（頓）我把所有T營的人名都記起來了。最近I營和P營的也彼此殘殺起來了。

碧：我不清楚欸。

（碧娜欲離開，但被莎夏拉住手。）

莎：我知道妳是誰。（碧娜頓住）所以，陪我聊聊吧。

（碧娜默默地坐回原位）

碧：妳是誰？

莎：我想先把I營和P營的事情說完，可以嗎？（碧娜不置可否地聳聳肩）妳有聽說過這兩個營發生了什麼事嗎？

碧：我不清楚。

莎：試著告訴我嘛，讓我知道妳了解多少。

碧：（思考了一下）因為有長官下令將 I 營和 P 營合併……。

莎：而 I 營和 P 營為了爭取有限資源和更大的活動區域而開始互相殘殺，是嗎？

碧：是。

莎：妳覺得是誰的錯？

碧：我不知道。

莎：I 營是最早被從地底世界翻上來迫害的，他們應該是最能理解被壓迫、被屠殺的感覺，如今他們只是繼續殘暴對待 P 營；不論在地下還是在這裡，人根本不會學到教訓。

碧：我不知道妳為什麼要跟我說這些。

莎：P 營的孩子痛苦的說「最安全的地方是墳墓」；那我們為什麼還要活著？

碧：（不安地）我想離開了。

莎：還記得拉轟嗎？

碧：偷東西後被砍斷四肢、丟入水池的那個。

莎：是為了替女兒醫病只好偷藥的那位；（頓）他被帶走前求我照顧他的孩子，我問他生活都這麼苦了，為什麼那時候不讓這個孩子死了算了？妳知道他怎麼回答我嗎？（碧娜搖頭）因為他相信這個孩子有一天、有一天能過著平凡快樂的日子，為了等待那天，他必須讓孩子活下去。

妳覺得這孩子等得到嗎？

碧：我不知道。

莎：那長官們會知道嗎？

碧：什麼？

莎：妳覺得什麼是平凡快樂？

碧：什麼長官？

莎：我覺得平凡快樂就是和愛的人在一起，不用遵守「不可離間、不可爭執、不可憤怒」，完完整整地做自己，離開集中營或是離開地下，自由選擇的生活。

碧：妳剛剛說什麼長官？

莎：不管在地下還是在集中營，我們其實都被管制、約束，沒有不同，只是一個比較強烈、一個比較和緩，妳能感覺到嗎？

（碧娜搖頭）

莎：這也是為什麼我們會落到這個地步，碧娜；我知道妳是誰嘟，妳是讓阿道夫長官活下來的人。

碧：我沒有。

莎：妳說讓大家決定他的死活，卻又拿長老的教誨來讓他活命。（頓）我還知道你們一家和他生活了一段時間，是嗎？（碧娜默不作聲，莎夏顯得有點激動。）果然是妳！真的是妳……。

碧：妳想幹嘛？

莎：我不會對妳怎麼樣，（笑）不可憤怒，對不對？（笑，接著念口訣般地重複著不可憤怒，直到回到一開始的狀態。），我家那區聽說有豐富的燃料礦產，所以當初全區的人直接被蕭清後丟在河裡流走，可是丟在河裡的人實在太多了，把整個河道稍稍地堵起來，我和我媽去拜訪親戚回來從下游往上走，只看到染紅的河水還有堆在窄河道、不斷互撞的屍體，我一眼就發現我的爸爸也在裡面；然後我們就被士兵帶來這裡，意外地活下來了。

碧：我聽好妳的故事了，我可以走了嗎？

莎：不；聽完我的請求我就走。

碧：妳說吧。

莎：我知道阿道夫長官一直想辦法再找妳；我也知道妳一直避著不想被發現，因為妳想贖罪；所以，我要妳被阿道夫長官找到，並且帶走我還

地下女子

116

有拉轟的孩子。

碧：這個⋯⋯。

碧：妳不是想贖罪嗎？

（碧娜遲疑）

莎：為了讓這孩子有一天能過著平凡幸福的生活，我要妳和阿道夫長官聯絡。

碧：是的。

莎：謝謝，等妳通知，我叫莎夏（欲離開）；對了，妳的媽媽還活著嗎？

碧：（猶豫一下）好吧，我知道了。

莎：真希望妳能體驗一下媽媽死掉的心情；阻止Ｃ區搶食物被射殺的楊花，就是我媽，妳知道嗎？

（莎夏離開，燈光變化。）

（歌曲）

噢～

知識的風暴

是非對錯你知了

情感的問答

誰能通達知曉

別說你知道

了解太表面

同感太敷衍

體會太做作

憐憫太倨傲

別說你知道

傷痛只有自己遭遇才明瞭

再多的話都無效

讓你是我　體會我內在的風暴

讓你是我　才不會只是表面的哀悼

如果你知道

不要再說話

就一個擁抱

石頭塔

媽：幼妹，在西口又發現上面掉下來的人，妳最近很常往西口跑；我很擔心……。

碧：媽媽……。

媽：發現地上人……。

碧：我知道。

媽：妳都知道，但是真的要做是很困難的。

碧：一定要用石頭把他們砸昏，確保他們昏了之後迅速回報對吧？

媽：妳不知道，幼妹，妳不知道，妳想得太簡單了；那是一個活生生的人，妳把一塊塊石頭往他身上砸的時候他會哀嚎、會求饒，或許妳會把他砸得遍體鱗傷，但他可能還有意識，妳要做的是讓他失去意識，妳得撿起一塊一塊的石頭往他身上丟，就算丟到他腦漿四濺也得做！

碧：我們一定要這麼野蠻嗎？

媽：幼妹！妳不了解上面的人有多恐怖就別指責自己的族人野蠻，他們屠殺我們，讓我們躲入地下，在這狹小的空間中苟活，但是他們依舊瘋狂地搜索我們，把所有可能像是我們出入口的洞穴填上，讓陽光再也照不進來。有人說，其他國家的人譴責地上人對地下人的殘忍，地上人卻說這個國家從來沒有過地下人；幼妹，現在的地下世界或許已經很舒服、很適合我們生活，但我們不能忘記地上人帶給我們的痛苦和血淚歷史。

碧：我不會忘記的。

（歌曲）〈石頭塔〉

石頭塔石頭塔

撿一顆石頭疊起來

把上面的破洞補起來

要小心　要小心

髒東西會掉下來

碰的一聲落下地

如果

還在喘　還在動

那就

讓石頭飛　把石頭砸

丟石頭不嫌累

聽到　停下來別理會

讓石頭一直飛　把石頭堆

直到只剩下石頭堆　哐哐響

丟石頭不嫌累

撿一顆石頭疊起來

石頭塔　　石頭塔

碧：媽媽，長老不是要我們不可爭執、不可離間、不可憤怒嗎？（頓）可
　　是為什麼我們要從小唱著這麼恐怖的歌？

媽：當妳全心全意的與人交往，妳確定別人也會一樣對妳嗎？

碧：當然不一定。

媽：尤其是恐怖的地上人。

碧：所以我們要一開始就抹煞他們？東洞的阿浪時不時就打罵他老婆、四
　　處拐騙，為什麼不拿石頭丟死他？

媽：他是我們地下人，不會犯下什麼滔天大罪的。

碧：即便他摔死他女兒？

媽：阿浪說是不小心的。

碧：不小心的孩子會摔到頭破血流？他分明就是對孩子施暴。

媽：不可離間。

（頓）

碧：媽！為什麼這時候妳又要搬出長老的教條來堵我的嘴。

媽：不可爭執。

（碧娜意欲噴發地不滿）

媽：不可憤怒。

（碧娜壓抑一陣，最後如同洩氣皮球般地垂下肩膀）

碧：東洞的阿浪時不時就打罵他老婆、四處拐騙為什麼不拿石頭丟死他？

媽：他是我們地下人，不會犯下什麼滔天大罪的。

碧：即便他摔死他女兒？

媽：阿浪說是不小心的。

碧：不小心的孩子會摔到頭破血流？他分明就是對孩子施暴。

媽：不可離間。

（頓）

碧：媽！為什麼這時候妳又要搬出長老的教條來堵我的嘴。

媽：不可爭執。

（停頓）

媽：不可憤怒。

碧：即便他摔死他女兒？

（碧娜感到壓抑）

媽：阿浪說是不小心的。

碧：不小心的孩子會摔到頭破血流？他分明就是對孩子施暴。

媽：不可離間。

（頓）

碧：媽！為什麼這時候妳又要搬出長老的教條來堵我的嘴。

媽：不可爭執。

（頓）

媽：不可憤怒。

（頓）

碧：媽媽，我只是很疑惑如果都不去討論前因後果，會進步嗎？

媽：討論也不一定會有進步，做好你自己份內的事。人家說棒打出頭鳥，記住，什麼事情都別衝得太前面，衝太前面只有被打的份，能交由別人決定的事就交給別人；但也別落得太後面，免得被淘汰掉。

碧：那如果大家都在中間呢。

媽：那就不會有人衝在前面、帶著我們衝在不對的路上、害我們被打，沒有人會帶來危險。

（靜默）

碧：媽，我帶回來一個地上人……他叫阿道夫。

（燈暗）

間奏 囈語

碧：（喘息著）呼呼呼，哈嘻。

A：妳可以幫我遞一下那個嗎？

碧：哪個？

B：蝸牛的慢跑鞋。

碧：星星。

C：掛在教鞭上，看到沒有？

A：那是猩猩。

B：關於蝸牛的慢跑鞋呢？

A：在左邊第九個抽屜。

C：不會圓滿。

碧：因為九嗎？

Ａ：對，因為九噢，沒有九會圓滿。

Ｃ：跟我說，呼喊。

碧：呼喊。

Ａ：你為什麼呼喊？

碧：為什麼呼喊？

Ｄ：獅子得不到牠的香蕉，正在生氣。

Ｅ：我們需要大象的蹼。

Ｆ：不好意思，今天的大象沒有蹼。

碧：那來一份尾巴。

沒有尾巴。

沒有理智。

沒有死亡。

Ａ：妳可以幫我遞一下這個嗎？

碧：哪個？

Ｂ：海牛的慢跑鞋。

Ａ：不是。

Ｂ：妳可以幫我遞一下這個嗎？

碧：哪個？

Ａ：妳的性命。

碧：我無法。

（燈暗）

自我介紹

（開始時，阿道夫從旁邊搬出一支帶有腳架的麥克風，碧娜儀態良好的。）

阿：阿道夫。

碧：碧娜。

阿：我已經死了。

碧：我不知道自己活著還死了。

阿：在我三十二歲那年，我拿著一把手槍對準自己的太陽穴自殺了。

碧：在我三十三歲那年，我和海倫娜、莎夏一起回到地底的故鄉。（對阿道夫）你為什麼自殺？

阿：因為選擇，因為妳們不敢選擇。

碧：嗯……其實是我們別無選擇啊；如果我們別無選擇，那也只好適應。

阿：所有事情都沒有選擇的權利？

碧：是。

（停頓）

阿：（嘆氣）我是來自胥納的阿道夫，作為發現地下世界並與之生活的第一人，而後又獲得國家栽培，以二十六歲的年紀成為地底開發部的最高執行人，同時也是我國史上最年輕的高階部長，除了遵循「開發地底獲得新資源」的終極目的外，同時也支援『疾病管制部』進行病理研究和相關實驗，提供「國家建設發展部」相關人力；（驕傲地）我遵循高層的的指令，以讓國家高度進步、發展為首要目標；以國家獲得最大利益為目標，我全力執行地下開發政策；國家的成功就是我個人的成功。（停頓，對碧娜。）妳了解國家優於一切嗎？

碧：嗯……都可以吧。

（靜默）

阿：妳相信救贖嗎？

碧：什麼？

阿：妳有仇恨嗎？對地上社會？

碧：如果別無選擇，那我們的仇恨又能怎麼辦？

阿：復仇呢？

碧：欸……那是我們全然不敢想像的事，我們要如何和整個地上社會為
　　敵。

阿：所以妳選擇任人擺佈？如果當初地底人發動抗爭，或許你們現在依舊
　　安然的活在地底。

碧：但……我們被從地底挖出來了，不是嗎？

阿：（激動）挖出來的時候為什麼不掙扎？！

碧：（思考）所以我們只能和死亡一起生活。

阿：現在也是？

碧：（笑）到現在我依然感覺到死亡就在我耳邊呼氣。

阿：而我是播種死亡的農夫。

碧：您十分盡責。

阿：是，我十分盡責。

碧：（笑）大家都說「在集中營沒有神，因為這裡可怕到連神也決定不來了」。

阿：看來我的盡責獲得空前的勝利。

碧：是的。

（靜默）

阿：莎夏恨妳嗎？因為我很常找你來。

碧：我盡量，盡量做到不讓她恨。

阿：很困難吧？

碧：因為……我們只剩彼此了吧。

阿：碧娜，妳怎麼可以如此…坦然？

碧：大概是因為可以抗議的時候我並沒有發聲，現在只能接受。

阿：任何處置妳都可以接受？

碧：（停頓）可以吧，沒有更慘的了；我待過集中營，看過兒子為了麵包可以將爸爸活活打死，看著為了讓自己不被槍射中而狂奔到將人踏死，活著跟死了也沒有太大的差別，都還好。

阿：看來集中營氣氛經營得不錯。

碧：是的。

（停頓）

阿：如果當初我沒有從集中營找到妳？

碧：那我現在大概跟著我母親一起長眠地下。

阿：現在這樣苟活著會恨我嗎？

碧：不會吧，我只能專注在當下，過去和未來都不是我有能力思考的。

阿：碧娜，妳是恨我的吧？請跟我說實話。

碧：阿道夫長官，我只會想接下來可能要做的工作，愛和恨不是我所能控制的……。

阿：阿道夫長官？妳叫我阿道夫長官……！好，我命令你回答我！妳恨我。

（靜默）

阿：妳恨我？

（靜默。碧娜絞盡腦汁的思考狀。）

碧：阿道夫先生，我只會想接下來可能要做的工作，愛和恨不是我所能控制的……。

阿：這樣能讓妳的仇恨消失嗎？

碧：我不知道。

阿：但是你恨我？（碧娜繼續思考，停頓。）所有地底人都唾棄我？

地下女子

136

碧：我不能代表他們。

阿：但妳也無法表達妳自己。

碧：（思考）那死亡是唯一解嗎？

阿：至少我選擇！對我來說是，因為該做決定的人遲遲沒有決定，重擔全都壓在我身上；真的很可悲呀，那些不敢做決定的人。（走到麥克風前）我是阿道夫。

碧：（微弱的）我是碧娜……。

（碧娜猶疑著，時而抿嘴時而嘆氣，欲言又止；像陷入沉思又像只是單純放空。一陣，阿道夫拿起麥克風往碧娜嘴邊送，碧娜迴避；兩人動作逐漸暴力直到阿道夫放棄將麥克風放回腳架。燈光漸暗至即將暗場，碧娜終於走到麥克風旁用手指輕敲麥克風。燈光回亮。）

（燈光等了一陣，發現碧娜沒有要繼續發言，燈暗。）

間奏 媽媽說

Ａ：碧娜。

碧：媽媽？是媽媽嗎？

媽：是的，我是媽媽；妳過得好嗎？

碧：媽媽，我過得很好。

媽：碧娜，妳記得媽媽說過什麼嗎？

碧：我記得媽媽說過的最後三日。

（停頓）

碧：媽媽，妳在嗎？

媽：碧娜，妳記得媽媽說過什麼嗎？

碧：媽媽，妳記得媽媽說過什麼嗎？

媽：媽媽說過最後三日親朋好友會回到身邊，回顧一生，重做決定。

媽：碧娜，妳記得媽媽說過什麼嗎？

碧：媽媽，最後三日親友們只會以聲音出現嗎？

媽：碧娜，妳記得媽媽說過什麼嗎？

碧：媽媽，妳記得媽媽說過什麼嗎？

媽：碧娜，要怎麼才知道最後三日來了？

碧：媽媽，妳記得媽媽說過什麼嗎？

媽：碧娜，妳記得媽媽說過什麼嗎？

碧：媽媽，妳已經被母神產下在新天地裡了嗎？

媽：碧娜，妳記得媽媽說過什麼嗎？

碧：媽媽，妳記得媽媽說過什麼嗎？

媽：碧娜，妳有遇到阿姑婆跟阿姑姨嗎？

碧：媽媽，你記得媽媽說過什麼嗎？

媽：碧娜，大家在那邊都還好嗎？

碧：媽媽，妳還記得媽媽說過什麼嗎？

媽：碧娜，我的最後三日開始了嗎？

碧：媽媽，妳還記得媽媽說過什麼嗎？

媽：碧娜，我們要來重做決定了？

媽：碧娜，妳還記得媽媽說過什麼嗎？

碧：媽媽，只有妳一個人來嗎？

媽：碧娜，你還記得媽媽說過什麼嗎？

碧：媽媽，我要怎麼準備最後三日？

媽：碧娜，妳為什麼不殺死阿道夫？

碧：媽媽，我們要開始⋯⋯！？

媽：碧娜，妳還記得媽媽說過什麼嗎？妳為什麼不殺死阿道夫。

（靜默，碧娜試圖呼喚媽媽幾次。）

碧：媽媽？（停頓）媽媽？（停頓）媽媽，我的最後三日什麼時候會來？

（靜默）媽媽？

A：我是阿道夫。

（燈暗）

終曲

（碧娜隨意地揮抬手，男人像將要煮沸的滾水般做著一些不明的動作，音樂混亂而爆裂，多焦並進。）

男：阿道夫！我等待的紅玫瑰，像鮮血，他們的荊棘，像枯骨；地底沒有星星，媽媽的眼睛沒有星星，只有染紅的溪水和漂浮的屍體；我一眼就看出來妳是牛，為什麼不逃！

碧：閉嘴。

男：因為我在等一朵玫瑰花；幼稚！阿道夫先生，幼稚！阿道夫先生，北風來了，幼妹！妳今晚要吃烤田雞腿還是我摔在地上爛掉的頭？

碧：紅色的。

男：巴掌大的蓮花打在屍體上，我會照顧妳和海倫娜的，寄生蟲，快帶妳的族人逃，騎著白蝸牛從濃煙中逃跑，變成岩壁上細細小小的花，再被刮下來。

碧：媽媽。

男：像個機器人、就像個機器人吃著棒棒糖，為了生活，看 I 營和 P 營瘋狂打炮，在旁邊搖旗吶喊，被打翻的半桶飯菜射入體內，用真空吸引，慢慢地轉；妳有看到我嗎？在黑暗中慢慢地轉，快點找到我。

碧：媽媽，妳還沒告訴我……。

男：長官，白魚，長官，田雞腿，長官，阿道夫，我等的只是一朵玫瑰；我寧願為了一顆糖果而活，像地下湖的浪。拉轟、拉轟！你的孩子、你的孩子，我不知道她有沒有過著平凡幸福的生活；媽媽、媽媽，妳是我的孩子……。

碧：媽媽，我的最後三日什麼時候會來？

男：不要怕，在選擇之前，早妳一步被母神產下、最親愛的朋友都會回到妳身邊，用三天的時間，最後三天一起和妳重新做一次決定。真的

地下女子

142

嗎？我們都在母神的肚子裡，我們只是在母神的肚腹裡等待產出；在此之前我們要不停地反芻是非對錯，把所有來自於情緒的決定都選擇過一次，等到我們做出最純粹的選擇，就會從母神的產道裡走出來，出生在新的世界裡。真的嗎？我不知道。真的嗎？我不知道。真的嗎？妳有選擇嗎？妳有決定嗎？妳敢選擇嗎？妳敢決定嗎？媽媽？媽媽？不要把我留在這裡……，最後三日要怎麼來？

碧：別說了。

（突然極其安靜，接下來對話兩人以一種極為冷靜，近似中性的方式對話。）

男：為什麼要阻止我。

碧：不想讓你說下去了。

男：為什麼不說？

碧：不可爭執、不可離間、不可憤怒。

男：為什麼不可。

碧：我不知道。

男：妳不知道，所以妳把災禍帶回地下世界。

碧：這是大家一起決定的。

男：因為妳不想當承擔責任的人；所以害大家被屠殺、被送進集中營，只剩下莎夏、海倫娜和妳被送回地下，妳的族人全都死去，因為妳什麼都沒做。

碧：我有，我有提出警告、我有曾經試圖要逃、我有參與抗爭。

男：妳只是把自己藏在裡面。

碧：那我應該要怎麼辦？

男：對，妳該要怎麼辦？

碧：找到罪惡的源頭。

男：誰？

碧：阿道夫。這一切都是你的錯。

男：是我的錯嗎？

碧：是你的錯。

男：所以讓我活下來是我自己的錯？沒有通報族人逃往北方是我的錯，沒有好好支持莎夏爭取留在地上社會的權利是我的錯，沒有撥出時間陪海倫娜聊美好回憶也是我的錯？妳的親人死絕、國家滅亡是我的錯。

碧：對！都是你的錯。

男：那妳要怎麼做？

碧：殺死阿道夫。（碧娜冷冷拿起刀子瘋狂的往男子身上戳刺，男子瞬間血如噴泉。）

男：（笑著）好痛呀，碧娜好痛呀。

女：不如嘗試如何真正的殺死我吧，（將刀子上安全膜剝除後，劈砍物品展示鋒利度後將刀鋒抵在脖子上。）這樣可以嗎？

碧：可以，你快殺死你自己。

（男人放下手中的刀，定定地看著碧娜；碧娜試圖做了幾個動作，男人重複；碧娜恍然大悟，一切僅是自己的想像，而後放棄。）

男：只有妳才能殺死妳自己。

（男人回到水中）

碧：（看向莎夏、海倫娜骸骨）妳們不會來找我對吧？（碧娜默默做了決定後往洞穴深處走去；燈光漸暗。）

（字幕：聽說碧娜在洞穴深處看到光亮，迎向她的是母神的新世界；她的媽媽、親人們都在那裡等著她，用笑臉和擁抱熱烈歡迎碧娜的到來；而莎夏、海倫娜和阿道夫，他們也在其中。燈暗。）

全劇終

劇場第八號年度製作

穢土天堂二部曲

地下女子

2014/09/26~28
臺北萬華糖廍藝文倉庫

《地下女子》二〇一四年曉劇場演出宣傳海報

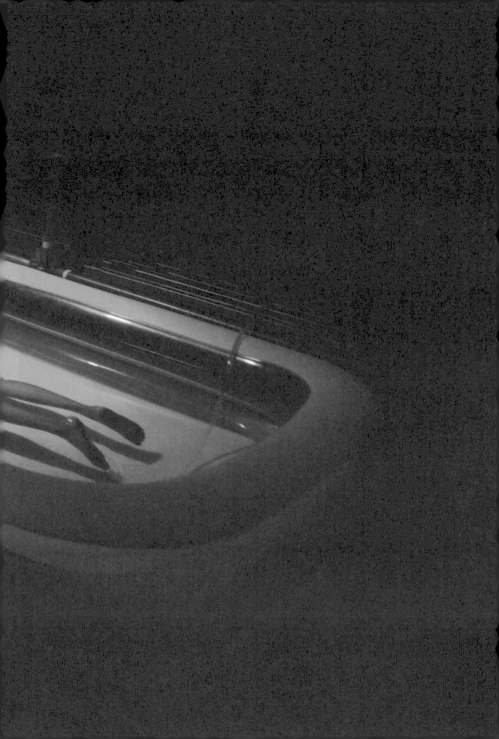

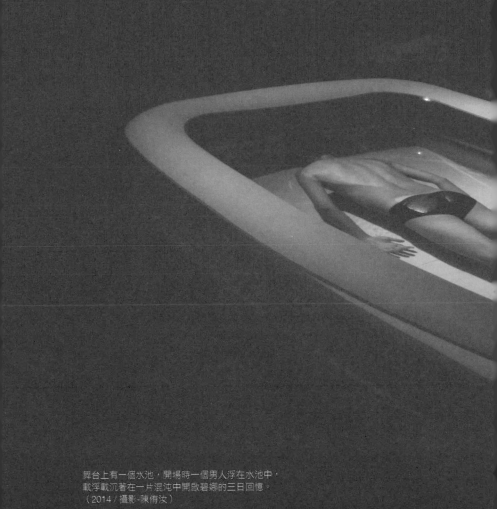

舞台上有一個水池，開場時一個男人浮在水池中，
載浮載沉著在一片混沌中開啟碧娜的三日回憶。
（2014 / 攝影-陳侑汝）

少年阿道夫偶然掉入地下後，與地底人
共同生活了一段時間，卻也為未來的不
幸埋下伏筆。（2014 / 攝影-陳侑汝）

始終接受各種命運遭遇的碧娜，在阿道
夫的質問下，面對自己間接讓地下世界
走向全面滅亡的實情。（2014 / 攝影-陳
侑汝）

海倫娜描述在集中營裡及地上世界中遭遇的各式性暴力，童言稚語的她令人可憐又可愛。（2014／攝影-陳侑汝）

屠殺地底人的行動開始後，阿道夫曾潛入地底村莊要碧娜趕緊逃跑，但卻被碧娜一口回絕。（2014／攝影-陳侑汝）

雞與牛的狂想，暗喻消極等待死亡到來的碧娜。（2014 / 攝影-陳侑汝）

集中營為了生存泯滅人性的種種慘
況，讓為了活下去的莎夏，利用碧
娜逃到地上世界成為示範女子。
（2014 / 攝影-陳宥汝）

碧娜違背了地底人須以石頭砸死外來者的規定，用地下世界的三戒律「不可憤怒、不可離間、不可爭執」使族人決定讓阿道夫活下來。（2014／攝影-陳侑汝）

※本書獲文化部贊助出版

國家圖書館出版品預行編目（CIP）資料

地下女子：穢土天堂二部曲 / 鍾伯淵著.
-- 初版. -- 臺北市：蔚藍文化, 2017.11
　面；　公分
ISBN 978-986-94403-6-3（平裝）

854.6　　　　　　　　　　106018717

CONTENTS

Underground Women-Paradise Lost

For this play, aside from the prelude and finale set to come first and last respectively, each individual skit may be performed in any random order or in accordance to the wishes of the actors.

Characters:

Pina (Cow, Mouse B)

Spirit (Adolf, Mother, Sasha, Helena, Aaron from the East Cave, Great Aunt, Chicken, Mouse A)

Singer

Musician

Scene: Non-specified space. There is a pool on stage. For the opening, a man is floating in the pool.

Prelude

(Opening: a man climbs out of the water.)

Spirit: What is this place? (pause) What is this place? (pause) Do you recognize it? If you do, then can you tell me what this place is, but do you recognize it? Do you recall? Will you recall? Do you dare to recall? Do you dare to endure? Or have you never recalled? Have you never once wondered, "Where am I?" "Why am I here?" or "What is going on here?".

You have never recalled, but let's be careful to avoid using the word "never." "Never" is too negative, which makes people resist it and deny it.

(one person plays two roles)

"I've never successfully lost weight."

"I've never thought of working earnestly."

"I've never liked my boss."

"I've never liked you."

"Really?"

(pause)

"I've never liked you either!" (extremely seriously then followed by a strong sense of being hit hard) Again! We must politely and gently say "maybe" you have not recalled. It's nothing to care too much about, because life for you has not changed. You use a simple "time flies" attitude to summarize your entire life experience. But in fact, you can't even share a single life image that has left a lasting impression on you .

Naturally, the word "numb" should not be used either, for it desecrates all you have experienced—even though you really can't say anything about anything and numbness itself makes people feel, well, numb! This is a place overflowing with sunshine and breezes filled with fragrances of fresh grass, that swoosh through the branches creating a most comforting rustling sound. (sudden storm sounds with wind and rain)

Maximum wind speeds of 150 kilometers per hour along with extremely heavy rain, rainfall in mountain regions

forecasted to break one thousand millimeters per hour, strong warnings for severe flash floods and landslides. (end sound effects, pause) Yes, soft breeze. We were talking about the soft breeze and green grass. See the green grass expand before your eyes with meadows split by springs and ripe fruit trees ready for picking. This is where we are.

(Song)

there is an immaculate piece of land

clean and pure to perfection

birds sweetly twittering in the trees

music flowing

and clouds floating about as colorful as a rainbow

the light leisurely turns

blissful heaven

a land bursting with colors

exploding with purples and reds

bees and butterflies fly

animals have no worries

there is a land so beautiful

there is a land so dreamy

there is a land we are so longing

we are so longing

Spirit: But actually, we are inside a whale's stomach. We live in a whale's stomach. Oh! What a poor life we live! We say this as we look towards the whale's mouth, anxious for all the food to pour in when it opens (huge water sounds, the man makes "tsk-tsk" sounds while meticulously sorting the food) Oh! All this old stuff again, how miserable! This is not good. Argh! My misery index is going off the charts! I can't handle this! (dumps pills from a bottle and carefully counts them, swallows the medicine and continues previous action) Oh, so painful. All this old stuff again, how miserable! I can't last much longer! (again dumps pills from bottle, carefully counts them, swallows) Oh! So tragic! All this old stuff again, how miserable! Oh! This is out of control! (again, grabs bottle, pauses, swallows whole bottle of pills, passes out on the ground) Resisting in every possible way, but preferring to hide and carelessly live in the whale's stomach, is that right? I am in trouble and I beg (covers mouth) that you answer me. I am calling

out from the depths of hell, please harken my voice. You cast me into the abyss, here in the deep sea, gulps of water surround me. Your waves overflow my body. I say, "Although I was expelled from your eyes, I still gaze towards your holy temple. All the water surrounds me, almost drowning me. The abyss imprisons me, seaweed wraps around my head. I approach the base of the mountain, the doors of the earth forever close upon me.

(Song)
This is the point of paradise
With the most beautiful scenery
This is a pure and beautiful land
With no evil
With no sin
This is the promised land
A land so beautiful with no sense of earthliness.
A land bursting with colors
Exploding with purples and reds
Bees and butterflies fly
Animals have no worries

Adolf: Pina (drags out sound) Pina, where are you?

Pina: (only voice) I am here. Quickly, come find me. Come find me!

Adolf: I can't see you.

Pina: (only voice) Just in the corner of your eye. I beg of you, let me stream down. Let me stream down, and you will find me. I have been lingering here for a long time.

Adolf: In the corner of whose eye?

(lights slowly dim and focus on Adolf)

Pina: (only voice) I……

Adolf: In the corner of whose eye?

Pina: (only voice) This……

Adolf: In the corner of whose eye? Hurry, tell me, so I may find you!

Pina: (only voice) Hurry, come find me.

Adolf: I will.

Pina: (only voice) But why do you want to find me?

Adolf: Because you wish to leave the darkness.

Pina: (only voice) Yes, I wish to leave the darkness. Please help
    me.

Adolf: I will

Pina: (only voice) What about Sasha? Where is she?

Adolf: She has left.

(light up two skulls)

Pina: And Helena?

Adolf: She has also left.

Pina: (only voice) They left together.

Adolf: Yes.

Pina: (only voice) Really? They left together?

Adolf: Yes.

(two girls with bright smiles appear in the back)

Pina: (only voice) Only I am left?

Adolf: Only you.

Pina: (only voice) You are still here, right?

Adolf: (hesitantly) You could say that, I am...... where are you?

Pina: (only voice) I don't know.

Adolf: You just said you were in the corner of whose eye? I will
    look for you next to them.

Pina: (only voice) I think I am in the corner of my own eye, but

I can't stream down.

(lights dim and instantly shine back on)

Pina: Mother, Mother.

Mother: What's the matter?

Pina: I can't get out.

Mother: Where can you not get out?

Pina: Everywhere. I am stuck in a predicament, and I don't know what to do. I can't make up my mind, but I don't want to not make up my mind.

Mother: If you wish to choose, then choose. All choices may be accompanied by mistakes.

Pina: I don't understand.

(lights change)

Aaron: I am Aaron from the East Cave! Tonight, would you like to have fried "cuisses de grenouille" or steamed whitefish?

Pina: Huh? (thinking) I would like both.

Aaron: But you can only choose one.

Pina: Then fried "cuisses de grenouille"

Aaron: But tonight's fried "cuisses de grenouille" might not be crispy enough.

Pina: Then steamed whitefish?

Aaron: The whitefish might be too fishy or too dry?

Pina: Then what should I do?

Aaron: We have not had whitefish in a long time.

Pina: Yes.

Aaron: I have heard that the whitefish is particularly plump and juicy lately.

Pina: Then let us have whitefish.

Aaron: You really want to have whitefish? Or only because of what I just said?

Pina: I am not sure.

Aaron: Choose the fried "cuisses de grenouille" then.

Pina: Wait, you said I could choose for myself, did you not?

Aaron: Then what do you want to have?

Pina: I would like the fried "cuisses de grenouille."

Aaron: Even though it might not be crispy enough?

Pina: Yes.

Aaron: And even though it might be too oily or not seasoned well enough?

Pina: It's okay.

(lights change)

Mother: You have made your decision. Even if this decision

does not bring you the goodness you might have imagined, but you have still made a decision towards a certain direction despite the points of disagreement, am I right? Maybe today's whitefish is unprecedentedly delicious and the fried "cuisses de grenouille" is unprecedentedly a failure. None of us know.

Pina: Then, Mother, do you feel we should have fried "cuisses de grenouille" tonight or steamed whitefish?

Mother: There is only stir fried potato root tonight.

Pina: Oh......

Mother: Sometimes even though you are allowed to make a decision, things still do not go in the direction you wish. Maybe both directions do not work, and it is the third or fourth or a better or worse path.

Pina: I don't know what to do anymore. Can I just stand still?

Mother: There is no still point, you will be pushed along.

Pina: But I have not made any decisions.

Mother: That is a decision in itself. We are all in the womb of Mother Earth. We are just in the womb of Mother Earth waiting to be born. Prior to this we must endlessly reflect on what is right and wrong, and reevaluate all the decisions

that came from emotions. When we finally make the purest decision, that is when we will make our way down the birth canal of Mother Earth and enter into a whole new world

Pina: Mother, how do I know when I will make the purest decision?

Mother: I have no idea.

Pina: I am afraid I will not be here for that day.

Mother: Do not be afraid. Before you decide, all your dear friends who are one step ahead of you and have already been born by Mother Earth will return to your side. Use three days' time. The last three days they will accompany you in remaking your decision.

Pina: Who will be these dearest friends? Who will be here by my side during the last three days? (silence) Sasha, will it be you? Helena, where are you? (pause) Mother? Are you still there?

(absolutely no reply)

Pina: Mother, you have not told me what the last three days look like? (pause) I am still waiting. Sasha? Helena? Where are you? Where are my last three days?

(Song)

Oh ~ last three days

Waiting to be surrounded

With those who have past

The unfortunate and unregrettable

Have all come before my eyes

To be together with dear friends

To revisit all the stories

During the last three days

Let me be surrounded by my own decisions

To be embraced together with my dear friends in the new world
by Mother Earth

But

Mother

You have not yet told me my last three days

How will they come?

(lights out)

Interlude: Action Sentences

(In this interlude, starting from the next bracket, all texts within brackets should be spoken by the narrator, with Pina moves accordingly.)

"Pina stands still."

"Pina stands still."

"Pina has no desires."

"Pina has no emotions."

"Pina has no actions."

"Pina has no thoughts."

"Pina has no life."

Pina: I am still alive.

"Pina still lives."

"Pina still waits."

"Pina is still numb."

"Pina still lives."

"Pina still lives numbly."

"Pina numbly lives and waits."

"Pina still numbly lives and waits."

Pina: Waiting for death to arrive.

"Pina waits for death to arrive."

"Pina waits for the last three days to arrive."

"Pina waits for deceased mother to arrive."

"Pina waits for deceased friends to arrive."

"Pina waits for deceased neighbors to arrive."

"Pina waits for deceased relatives to arrive."

"Pina waits for deceased classmates to arrive."

"Pina waits for deceased Sasha to arrive."

"Pina waits for deceased Helena to arrive."

"Pina waits for her own death to arrive."

Pina: Pina waits for her own death to arrive.

"Death does not arrive."

Helena

(Helena wears a fluffy tutu and sits on the ground with legs spread open. She moves a stick in and out of her mouth with dull eyes, while talking to Pina)

Helena: Oh, oh, yuck.

Pina: (folding flowers) Just keep it in your mouth. Don't use force. Use your head to spin. When you spin, the stick will do the same in your mouth.

(Helena does as instructed, after spinning for a while.)

Helena: Yuck. Sister, my head is spinning.

Pina: You're swinging too big. Plus you're going to injure your teeth with scratches that way and whip your face.

Helena: Oh. (Stops what she's doing and stares off into space. Pina watches for awhile.)

Pina: Hey, why are you stopping? Vacuum suction, have you learned it?

(Helena shakes her head)

Pina: Such a primary skill and you still have not learned it. How will the senior officials be happy about this? (guiding Helena) Come here. Place this shallowly in your mouth. Suck in, yes, oral contraction will cause a vacuum effect. (Helena sucks too hard. The whole stick went into her mouth. She is nauseated.) No, not too deep. (Helena shallowly puts stick in mouth and sucks) Yes, you've finally got it. That's right.

Helena: I got it.

(Pina continues to fold flowers. Helena continues to practice "vacuum suction" and begins humming a song.)

(Song)
<Going Round in Circles>
Turn, turn, around in circles
Put the stick in your mouth and stir
Gently shake your head and nod your brain
Turn too briskly, head will get dizzy
Gently around, round in circles
vacuum~ suction.
Hum hum hum, no stick eat whip

Hot hot spicy spicy
Blossom a flower
Hum hum hum, ho ~

(Helena slowly loses momentum, stops work again)

Pina: Helena.

Helena: Sister, I want to eat roasted hamster.

Pina: Mhm.

Helena: Cover the hamster with a thick layer of rock salt and roast it with yams and hot stones. (sings) So ~ delicious.

Pina: That is not hygienic.

Helena: You think so? Sister, have you never had that before?

Pina: (shakes head) I have.

Helena: (laughing and singing) Crunchy crunchy roasted hamster, salty and crispy. (speaking) Sister has had it before, but you find it unhygienic now? How come?

Pina: (stops folding paper, sternly says) You should keep practicing (pause) Are your legs lifted high enough in the front? Don't inconvenience the senior official's entrance. What about doggy style? Is your bottom lifted high enough? Your waist pressed down? This is will help you stay tighter.

Helena: Oh.

(Pina continues to fold flowers, long pause)

Helena: Sister, have you had ferns before? (Pina shows no reaction) What about Sister Sasha?

Pina: She went to see if Senior Official Adolf needed any help with anything.

Helena: How can someone dislikes resting time so much?

Pina: Resting time is left for people who have abundance in time.

Helena: What is "abundance?"

Pina: It is when you finish practice and work and still have your own free time.

Helena: Then I cannot not have abundance? (pause) But Sister Sasha has already completed her work very well, why does she go to Senior Official Adolf looking for more work?

Pina: (long pause) I don't know.

Helena: Oh, then when will I have my own abundance in time?

Pina: When you have practiced well. Responsibility, Responsibility.

Helena: Hm. Mhm. Then I am never going to have abundance in time! Sister Sasha either.

Pina: Why not?

Helena: Senior Official Adolf is very busy. Sister Sasha will have much to help him with, especially since Sister Sasha is mostly busy being around Senior Official Adolf.

Pina: That doesn't count as helping.

Helena: Oh! (suddenly thinks of something) Ferns are really delicious! I have only had it once. Mother said she picked it by Face Day Creek, she said she secretly picked it, because if any elders discovered she went out into the open sky, she would surely be scolded. Crispy and sticky and so tasty, even with a hint of grass flavor.

Pina: Helena.

(long pause)

Helena: Sister, I wish to go home.

Pina: Go home?

Helena: Go home. I want to have delicious white snails. Every year for my birthday Mother would roast fresh rosemary with white snails. She would go to the east valley to gather fresh rosemary, brown and green rosemary with a hint of sweat and chokingly spicy flavor—a magical powder filled with fragrance. And if you use twigs collected from the

banks of the underground Cloud Creek to create a thick white smoke, it will give a smoky flavor to the plump and juicy white snail meat, which would be charred with a slightly salty texture of rosemary, and along with that smoky flavor......

Pina: Don't say it anymore.

Helena: W-H-Y? I want to go home. I miss Mother.

Pina: Learn to grow up will you? Helena, don't act like a child and avoid what you must do.

Helena: I am a child.

Pina: But you are not anymore. Now you don't have Mother to care for you. She is dead. So she will no longer be cooking white snails for you on your birthday, do you understand?

Helena: (starts to cry) Why must you be so mean? Of course I know Mother is dead, because she was killed right in front of me. Poor Mother ...

Pina: Helena.

(Helena mumbles something incomprehensible)

Pina: Helena.

Helena: Her eyes were wide opened staring straight at me. Her eyes were already starless, there was only red water flowing

and flowing.

Pina: Helena, don't say it anymore.

Helena: How can I not say anything? When I talk about this I can reminisce about feeling good or bad. Only then can I own the feeling that I am still alive.

Pina: But talking about it does not make up for anything. It is useless! What is the point of talking when things cannot be resolved? What is the use of reminiscing? thinking?

Helena: I don't know what is the use either...... talking about it makes me angry. I cannot let it go. So I think about what I can do, and how can I do? Because I don't want to continue living like this. I don't .

Pina: That is not possible.

Helena: If you don't do it, how do you know it is not possible?

Pina: Be good, please listen to me, will you? Would you like some candy? (Helena shakes head) Right now just focus on doing what you must do and leave the rest behind.

Helena: What are the things I must do?

Pina: Serve the senior officials well.

Helena: Even if I don't like it?

Pina: (gently) Even if you don't like it.

Helena: What about the other things?

Pina: The other things are not important right now.

Helena: This is like being a robot.

Pina: That is life, you know.

Helena: We are all robots.

Pina: That is life.

(Helena sings while she moves)

(Song)

<Sour and Tart Song>

Hum hum hum yo~

Tilt up

Press down

Body needs to know how to wriggle

Mouth licks a never melting lollipop

Smelly (laughs)

Smelly

Flip over

Lift up

Sour and tart

Body eats lemons

Sour and tart

Eyes are sour, too

Helena: This is work?

Pina: This is work.

Helena: Why must we work?

Pina: To exchange place to live, clothes to wear and the food to
eat.

Helena: Even if I don't like it.

Pina: Yes, it is for survival.

Helena: I would rather live for a piece of candy.

Pina: Candy? (takes out a piece of candy) Want it?

Helena: Not this kind. Those are considered … for work (laughs)
but not for survival.

Pina: I don't understand what you are saying.

Helena: When I was at the concentration camp (Singer begins
to sing "Sour and Tart Song") there was a security guard
uncle. He would come see me every few days. Every time
he would give me a piece of candy. At night, very later, he
would say, "Little girl, uncle gives you candy to eat, want
it?" The candy had a variety of flavors—sweet or sour.

Pina: (folding flowers) Wow, the uncle was nice to you. You had candy to eat in there.

Helena: He would always play a game with me, play a silent game. "The candy is very good, right? So slowly you must let it melt until it has completely dissolved in your mouth. You must not bite it to pieces at once. And you must not accidentally swallow it or spit it out." The uncle would play a game called question-and-answer with me. "What is your name?" (shakes head) "Where are you from?" (shakes head) "Where are your parents?" (shakes head) "What do you like to eat the most?" If I...... (immediately covering mouth, revealing a winning smile) passed the test, uncle would push the stick inside just like the senior officials.

Pina: How could you let him do that?

Helena: Because it was a game.

Pina: That is wrong.

Helena: He would slowly press on my body, checking if the candy was still in my mouth while lightly touching me, whispering in my ear: to be good, be good, and little by little he would push the stick inside.

Pina: Concentration camp does not allow such a thing. You

should have reported him.

Helena: It was just a game. The uncle always said I did well, and I really liked it. I liked being praised and eating candy. I liked the uncle softly whispering words in my ear. I liked that the uncle was like the waves of the underground, wave after wave gently pushing me.

Pina: (covers Helena's mouth) Don't say it anymore.

Helena: This one neither?

Pina: This is illegal.

Helena: Why? The senior officials do the same thing to me, so they are not breaking the law?

Pina: They are different people. Senior officials never break laws.

Helena: But the uncle was very good to me. Every time I think about that game, it is like I can taste the sweet fragrant flavor of the candy. The senior officials only make me cry in pain. The senior officials like to see me cry, but I don't like to cry.

Pina: Senior officials are the boss, so we must do what senior officials like. That is our job. We do it for food, shelter and clothing.

Helena: I would rather to have only a piece of candy.

Pina: I would rather you did it for survival, for practicing.

Helena: More practices, pain and tears.

Pina: Dear Helena, no one likes tears. And tears cannot help you with anything. So, don't shed any tear. Live a good life.

Helena: Live a good life.

(Helena trembles, hiding emotions while practicing. Pina folds flowers.)

Interlude: Stone Tower

(Song)

Stone tower, stone tower

Pick up a stone and pile it up

Fill any holes on it

Be careful, be careful

Dirty things will fall down

Falling to the ground with a bang

If

Still panting, still moving

Then

Let the stones fly, smash the stones

Never get tired of throwing stones

If something is heard, stop, stop and ignore

Let the stones continue to fly, pile the stones

Until only a pile of stones is left, bang bang bang

Never get tired of throwing stones

Pick up a stone and pile it up

Stone tower, stone tower

(Lights go out)

Discovering Adolf

(16 year old Pina)

Pina: Who is that in the dark?

(lights change, slightly dark on stage Pina is carefully cautious)

Male: Anybody there?

Pina: Who are you?

Man: Please help me.

Pina: Where are you?

Man: Just keep walking forward and you will see me. Please help me.

Pina: Where are you?

Man: I'm here.

Pina: Where are you?

Man: Keep walking forward.

Pina: Where are you? I don't see you.

Man: I'm in the dark, look carefully.

(lights darken, man's voice repeats and becomes more and more hollow in sound)

Pina: I can't find you.

Man: Walk further into the darkness a bit. Do you see me? I'm in the dark. It's not that easy to see me, like a disaster. Disasters don't appear in daylight, only hidden in the dark waiting for opportunity to attack. That's me. Have you found me yet? Please help me. I've broken my leg and can't walk.

Pina: I'm already in the darkness, but I still can't find you.

Man: Further in, in the core of darkness—a place your subconscious avoids contacting. Can you see me?

Pina: I can't find you. Can you hear my voice and move closer to me?

Man: Disaster does't take the initiative to move close to people, but if you desire and call out for it, it will appear.

Adolf: My leg is broken, I can't move.

Pina: Make some sound, let me know where you are?

(out comes an ominous feeling of repeated sounds)

Man: You know disaster will bring destruction, why do you still look for it in the dark? Let it die. Let it die. Let it die. Let it

die...... (each sentence overlapping the next)

(Song)
<Naughty Darkness>
Darkness is naughty
"Ya oh~Ya yo~" so naughty
Intangible joy
But still mystically charming
Naughty darkness
Tank to your heart's desire
I'm about to step into darkness
Enjoy naughty darkness
Collapsing stimulus
Mother says don't use force with darkness
For you can't control it
But "ya yo yo" I love the naughty darkness.
The thrill of adventure

(music finishes, return to sheer silence)

Pina: Don't worry, I have almost found you. How did you get
    hurt?

Adolf: I fell into a cave. I called for help for a long time, but no one has come to save me. So, I tried to climb out, but discovered another pathway instead. Therefore, I continued to crawl along it. Have you almost found me?

Pina: Keep talking. I have almost found you.

Adolf: Originally I was able to crawl, but it got higher and higher, as if someone had built something. At first, I thought it was an abandoned mine of some kind. Then, I thought, could this be the legendary path to the underground?

Adolf: Have you found me yet?

Pina: I see you.

Adolf: Looks like I'm saved (Pina lifts a rock) I never imagined there would really be people underground! I have discovered the underground, discovered underground people! This discovery will surely shock the world.

Pina: Why are you not moving?

Adolf: I think I broke my leg. I can't move. You will help me to your village for treatment, will you? I can't see where you are. It's so cold here. I'm in such pain and discomfort.

Pina: Who are you?

(Pina raises the stone high. Lights change.)

Adolf: I'm Adolf of Xu Na.

(Lights dim. Music plays depicting the ripple turmoil in Pina's heart. Whether to kill Adolf or not seesaws in her brain with Mother's serious reminder. A chaos of wanting to interact with a new life superimposed with the aged familiarity of the old life. Actor as silhouette in the dark frozen in the pose of Pina holding up the stone then extremely slowly putting down the stone)

Adolf: Why did you put down the stone back there?

Pina: I don't know.

Adolf: Even though you take me back, the others will still form a stone tower around my body?

Pina: Some people certainly want to and some don't. So, I asked the elders what about our "no disputing, no alienating, no anger?" Why can everyone split and hold hatred over someone from aboveground?

Adolf: And then...... ?

Pina: Then you were let go.

Adolf: If you were asked the same question, how would you answer?

Pina: (Unconvincing shrug) I have no idea and don't wish to

prove anything. I just feel, "I don't want to make a decision and kill this person before me." But I could not just leave you there, since this is not a matter that can be so easily ignored.

(Long pause. Adolf concentrates on Pina. Pina turns her head away, sudden change.)

Pina: This is my secret little cave. No one has ever been here before.

Adolf: Why are you letting me see this?

Pina: Do you like it?

Adolf: Very pristine and full of life.

Pina: Whenever I'm in a bad mood, I will come to this small cave and vent my emotions. This is my outlet even though it's obviously just a small cave. It's very amazing. What do you think?

Adolf: I think it's definitely wonderful, but I can't relate.

Pina: I like this moist, warm feeling. I'm so thirsty. Are you thirsty?

Adolf: I'm fine.

Pina: (Takes out bottle and attempts to take out the cork.) I'm so thirsty! Mhm. Mhm. Ah.

Adolf: Let me try. (Takes bottle and tries to remove the cork.) Oh, I can't. If we can't open it, then forget it.

Pina: I'll try again (takes back bottle) Oh...... it's so tight...... so tight.

Pina: Can we really do this?

Pina: Does't matter, It's just so tight.

Adolf: Is it still so tight?

Pina: I think it has loosened a little.

Adolf: Then is it coming out yet?

Pina: It's loose. It's loose. (hand bottle to Adolf) Can you feel it?

Adolf: I think it's really not that tight anymore.

Pina: Then I will continue.

Adolf: Mhm.

Pina: Ah! Ah! Ah! Almost there! Almost there! (the cork is pulled out) Oh! It came.

Adolf: It finally came. You must be so tired.

Pina: I'm fine.

Adolf: (pause) If back then my body was made into a stone tower, what would you have done?

Pina: (shaking her water bottle) Then I would be so thirsty to

death by now. (Pina drinks water.)

Adolf: I did not help you with anything, like a useless handicap.

Pina: You staying with me is enough.

Adolf: Really? (long pause) Do you still remember the flower I taught you to roll?

Pina: Mhm.

Adolf: That's my favorite flower. It's called a rose. Roses come in many colors, but I feel a real rose must be red. Their stems have prickly thorns, so they bloom as if to lure people closer, yet insult people with a briery refusal.

Pina: Are you a rose?

Adolf: (shakes head) I'm only Adolf. (pause) I'm going back soon. One day I may return to the underground. I will bring a rose to see you.

Pina: Before then, I will keep rolling roses to wait for you.

(silence)

Adolf: Why did you save me then?

Pina: I didn't save you. Like I said before, I just simply didn't want to make a decision.

Adolf: But you bringing me back for the masses to decide on my life was a decision, was it not? (Pina stunned) Do you

regret it?

Pina: I miss everyone.

(lights go out)

Interlude: Mice

(two people wearing mouse masks stand on stage, motionless)

Music: Trash mountain. Complicated, irregular, uncoordinated and abrupt. Similar to an ode to life—but using filth and corpses and hard-on-the-ear insults instead. Vibrant colors of trash to make a hovering tower, but there are small objects falling constantly. Looking carefully, one may discover many spaces that are simple and crude but good for nesting.

Stage:This is the world's compost point. People become minuscule walking inside—as small as maggots drilling in the channels. They have also built a few places where smoke rushes straight to the horizon. The original black and grays have long been unrecognizable while birds circle the chimneys. Compared to the silently exploration drilling

adults, there are skinny dogs with their pointing tails running around small people who were called children.

(Music strongly takes up space, only when looking carefully you can discover A has an excited expression. B is growing in difficulty. B is about to fall but straightens up right away. A, on the other hand crawls like an animal on the ground, but after noticing B standing in silence. A also stands and adjusts her poses until they are exactly like B. Silence. A sometimes moves with impatience, but instantly returns to aforementioned pose. Then a few times A dances crazily under the influence of music. B remains well-mannered but is slowly losing patience, finally walks toward the microphone.)

B: No …

A: (imitates B) No.

B: No music.

(music ends)

A: Music no good?

B: No.

A: Mhm. (music randomly starts again as if it is unable to restrain)

B: But…… no music.

(music ends)

A: Why not?

B: First of all, I respect your enjoyment and your right to listen to music, and I will also not judge any of the noisy, harsh, making-one-impatient, rubbish music you listen to. Actually, I would not mind listening to more, but not right now.

A: Then when?

B: When the time comes, you will know.

A: Eh, do you like?

B: Like what?

A: Me.

B: You?! You are so dirty and covered with germs.

A: Am I?

B: And you look wretched.

A: Eh?

B: How can you let yourself wallow in degeneration?

(A starts playing around with the sound of "wallow in degeneration")

A: You do not like our music?

B: No.

A: There is nothing you like?

B: Please, of course not.

A: How come?

B: You are a mouse!

A: You too.

B: I refuse to admit I am a wretched, filthy, vulgar dirty mouse.

A: Why?

B: Because I have been educated.

A: Education will change the fact that you are a mouse?

B: Education will change my perspective.

A: You look down on other mice?

B: I did not say that.

A: But that is how you are acting.

B: I respect you, but that does not mean I understand you.

A: Then does that respect not seem fake?

B: I am the mouse who has been educated. What gives you the
   right to talk like you have such great knowledge?

A: I do not know.

B: Very good. Now please take your music and your dirty,
   vulgar lifestyles and get out of here.

A: Leave you alone here?

B: Yes, leave me alone.

A: This way, you will not be lonely?

B: I need an elegant, clean environment to live.

A: What about the other mice?

B: They can choose to be just like me or be phased out. Only those who are at my high level may be good enough to live and converse with me.

A: You have a pointy nose.

B: Yes.

A: And two big front teeth.

B: Mhm.

A: But where did your education go wrong?

B: What?

A: It has made you forget who you are, Pina.

(lights go out)

Sasha

(Pina folds flowers while looking at Sasha and Helena's remains)

Pina: If you two were still alive, what would you say to me? Like "Today, let us go to the creek and catch whitefish." or "Cook a few white snails for Helena." Words such as these? I eat whatever now that I am one person, Helena, your favorite white snails can be found everywhere now, no one will fight with you for them. You will not need to wait until your birthday to enjoy some. Sister, I, can bake them for you anytime you want. Your mother used to collect rosemary moss using a scraper to lightly scrape off the finest powder, right? Sister, I, can generously slab on a thick layer of rosemary moss. No one is collecting them. What was that? Whitefish, you say? (laughs) It's been a long time since I had whitefish. A year ago I saw a camera crew by the creek that belonged to the aboveground people, saying that

they were looking for the last of the underground people. I didn't want to be too obtrusive. I stuck to my fair share of things, so I seldom went back, lest I encountered them again. But Sasha, if you saw them, you would definitely rush forward, wouldn't you?

Sasha: Wouldn't I what? (Pina, somewhat taken back, can't believe Sasha is really responding to her. Sasha laughs while walking out carrying a plate of fruit) What are you doing?

Pina: (stutters) Where have you been?

Sasha: I went to help Mr. Adolf, where else?

Pina: How come you kept me waiting for so long?

Sasha: Have you lost your mind? Where is Helena?

Pina: I don't know.

Sasha: You don't know? Did you not say you were going to help keep an eye on her? You never learn and just hang around all day. If you don't perform well, you will cause trouble for Mr. Adolf.

Pina: Is that so?

Sasha: How could it not be so? Can you not spend all day just folding those flowers in your hand? Hurry and look for

Helena! I need to rest a bit. Being by Mr. Adolf's side is too exhausting, staring at a poker face all day. Ask him something, he never answers. Help him do something, he never shows gratitude. I absolutely can't take it anymore, let alone others. (pause) What are you still staring at? Go find Helena!

Pina: Will you still be here when I return?

Sasha: What crazy talk are you talking about? Of course I will not be here.

Pina: Where are you going?

Sasha: Lady, have you been so high with the senior officials, that you have fried your brains? Other than Mr. Adolf's, where else could I go?

Pina: Must you go?

Sasha: That goes without saying! Without me do you think he can get anything done?

Pina: Can you stay with me?

Sasha: Crazy girl, stay with you for what?

Pina: Stay with me and help me decide on a few things.

Sasha: Pina, I have no interest staying and helping you decide on anything. Can you not just decide on your own? Besides,

other than your job of folding flowers, you have nothing else to do, really? Don't bother me with such things, please?

Pina: Adolf is that important?

Sasha: (Full pause) Adolf, Adolf, you should add "mister" before his name. I don't care how close you were before, remember your place now.

Pina: Then why do you keep pestering him?

Sasha: Why? You want me to be here folding flowers like you? Or living life as a person who once had a good friendship with Mr. Adolf? Don't be a blood-sucking insect, will you?

Pina: Do your fair share, Sasha. Our job is to service the senior officials. You keep running to Mr. Adolf all day, are you not afraid he will become angry?

Sasha: Mr. Adolf is beyond happy to have me. (pause) Pina, if you don't mind, we can go together.

Pina: Sasha.

Sasha: What?

Pina: You don't think this is too ostentatious?

Sasha: Ostentatious? How is this ostentatious?

Pina: Throwing yourself at Mr. Adolf all day?

Sasha: Are you jealous?

Pina: What are you talking about?

Sasha: (lifts breasts and pushes down on lower part) How long do you think I can depend on these? Yes, indeed, to outsiders we appear to be the finest among underground people, attending shows and programs. We seem to have accepted the education of the aboveground people, but in reality, we are just toys for the senior officials. I don't need to remind you of this, do I?

Pina: No.

Sasha: Then how long do you think the senior officials will fancy us? Or do you think the TV shows and radio programs will just keep airing? This society will lose interest in us sooner or later. What will you have left then? Going on programs to talk about Dadaism, fauvism, pastoral, abstract aesthetic bullshit? Or do you wish to return to a long ago destroyed underground? (gets emotional) A policy made by Mr. Adolf (points at Pina) who singlehandedly led in the destruction of the underground.

(Sasha stops, calms down a bit)

Sasha: No use in bringing up the past no matter how many times. I wish to diligently live in this society aboveground.

One day when there will be no senior officials, no eyes on me any longer, I will still be able to live on. (pats Pina's face) When that time comes should I need to support you and Helena, I think I can. (yanks the flower from Pina's hand) When that time comes I want you to decorate a whole wall with flowers, the kind that are like splattered paint and teeny tiny expanding specs. (leaves Pina, but suddenly turns head around) And also, Mr. Adolf will one day smile at me. (throws flower away in a parabolic arch).

Pina: Sasha.

Sasha: What?

Pina: If you did not launch a protest march, would we still be able to stay aboveground?

(lighting changes into a malaise, weak feeling)

Sasha: (suddenly weakens, loses strength) The seniors decided to send us back, didn't they?

Pina: But maybe if they saw how obedient we were, they may once again relent.

Sasha: Do you think they would be so kind?

Pina: You made the protest march too big.

Sasha: I did that so the three of us could survive up here

aboveground—the last three people from the underground.

Pina: I know.

Sasha: After Mr. Adolf killed himself, we can only depend on ourselves. Mr. Adolf, who treated us the best, carried all the infamies and sins to commit suicide. (laughs coldly) Saying that, "Let underground people return to their world." We lost everything long ago.

Pina: Ever since we were first sent aboveground until we were repatriated, you have always remained so positive.

Sasha: What are you trying to say?

Pina: As a surviving person of the underground, don't you feel you are being too strong?

Sasha: Was it wrong of me to fight? Was it wrong of me to do something for myself? My home all smashed, family all killed. Why be so cruel to make me come back and face all this? Is it wrong to wish to stay aboveground? Is it cold blooded? Does it mean I don't love my hometown?

(Sasha starts to cough severely)

Pina: Sasha, are you okay?

Sasha: I have to go.

Pina: Where are you going?

Sasha: I feel like my last three days are coming.

Pina: Don't go.

Sasha: I must go.

Pina: I beg of you, don't leave me or Helena behind.

Sasha: We return again to Mother Earth's belly. I will help you two see what the new world looks like.

Pina: Will you, during the last three days, change any of your previous decisions?

Sasha: No, not a single one.

(After Sasha finishes, her whole body collapses on the ground; Pina madly shakes Sasha)

Pina: Sasha! Sasha! Don't go! Don't make any decisions and there will be no last three days! No! No! Sasha! Where are my last three days? Sasha!

(Man opens his eyes, reaches over and gives Pina a crisp slap across the face)

Man: I am Adolf.

(lights go out)

Interlude: Chicken and Cow

(this part begins with a clear and slow state, but gradually evolving into a strong and erosive state.)

Chicken: bok bok bok, bogok.

Cow: Moo ~ oh.

Chicken: bok bok bok, bogok.

Cow: Moo ~ oh.

(cow chews the cud)

Chicken: Bogok ... bok bok bok, bogok.

(cow chews the cud)

Chicken: Cluck cluck cluck (struts back and forth) bok bok bok, bogok.

(cow chews the cud)

Chicken: bok bok bok

(cow chews the cud, chicken struts back and forth)

Cow: Chicken, what are you looking for?

Chicken: Death.

Cow: Moo ~ (continues to ruminate)

Chicken: Cow, what are you waiting for?

Cow: Death.

Chicken: Bogok, bogok. How many ways can a cow die?

Cow: (puzzled) Huh?

Chicken: We have tens of thousands of chickens, but only one way to die.

Cow: I understand, moo ~~~

(chicken stretches its neck out, feet kicking, next making a gargle sound with fading chicken sounds, next as if it were thrown into boiling water, then a feather removal machine. Chicken turns while making clunk clunk sounds. Its body clangs and clashes in the roller; repeat many times. Cow chews while watching. Chicken vomits.)

Cow: Dizzy?

Chicken: Not really, actually. A chicken turns once in a lifetime. Bok bok bok, bogok.

(chicken pretends to make a noose and throws it around the cow's body)

Cow: My turn, moo.

(Chicken takes cow around to a set point, takes rope in hands, ties it to the ground, and brings a big and heavy hammer from afar. Cow makes mooing sounds, but does not move and stays in place. Chicken calculates route of trajectory, making marks back and forth. Cow stays still and watches chicken. Chicken takes the hammer and thumps the cow on the head. Cow falls on the floor shaking head and swinging all four limbs. Cow goes up and uses a knife to slit the cow's throat. Cow makes mooing sound, chicken sits back and watches.)

Chicken: bok bok bok ~ bogok, bok bok bok ~bogok (long pause) Why did you not escape, Pina?

The Message

(Pina rolls flowers in her hand, as if she hears something, stops in mid-action. Certain of no sound, she continues to fold flowers. Suddenly stops and jumps up. Immense sounds and lights abruptly coming from afar with vibrations transmitting through the rocks. Slight sounds of people's voices accompanied with shocking echoes bouncing back and forth forming a certain bizarre rhythm like crying in harmony, chanting, "Slaughter is forming afar." Pina mouths the words, "stone tower")

Adolf: Pina.

(Pina stops chanting "stone tower" solidifying under colossal music and lights and uses a strange expression to look at Adolf, then in a crazy manner roars the word "Adolf!" Music and lights, like the receding tide, fades far away)

Pina: Adolf, (give Adolf the flower in her hand) look! I am rolling flowers.

Adolf: Pina….

Pina: Look at how many flowers I have folded. After you left, I have been thinking about us going to flower valley to see flowers, thinking about the rose you mentioned. You taught me. I have rolled one after another. Everyone likes them and asks what this beautiful flower is called. Everyone says, "Pina, the next flower is for me." Everyone gives me paper, gives me fabric, for me to make roses. Everyone compares which rose is more beautiful. So many girls have learned from me how to make a rose. Their mothers say, "This is Pina's rose, don't bother her. Wait for her to roll for us, please?" Actually, I can teach them how to roll.

Adolf: Pina, Xia Nan district invasion has begun! There is still time now to escape. Go back and tell the elders, quickly lead everyone to escape.

Pina: Then, then from Isaeai district we are discovered by the people aboveground. The invasion begins. The people who escaped to the north says they are led by someone from the world aboveground, who's leading an army……

Adolf: Pina, I know you have much you would like to say, but this is not the time to reminisce.

Pina: People are killed, their bodies piled up as high as a
  mountain. People are taken away...... it is said that they
  will be used for hard labor.

Adolf: Pina, I know how the armies will treat you all, so please
  quickly escape, will you?

Pina: All the roses that were adorned on heads, pinned on
  chests, hung by doors have all been torn down one by one
  and thrown to the ground. I don't have any more material
  waiting to be rolled. Everyone knows the one who has led
  the invasion of the underground is "Adolf"

Adolf: Adolf.

Pina: Adolf.

Adolf: Adolf.

Pina: Adolf.

Adolf: Adolf.

Pina: Adolf.

Adolf: Adolf.

Pina: Adolf.

Adolf: Adolf.

Pina: Adolf.

Adolf: Adolf.

Pina: Adolf. (two begin to laugh) Adolf, you made me wait so long. Look at the roses I have rolled, do they look like the real thing?

Adolf: Yes.

Pina: I have been folding roses this whole time. That day in flower valley, you said the next time we meet you would bring a real rose for me, did you bring one?

Adolf: Sorry, Pina.

Pina: You forgot? That is fine. (covers face and opens again) Adolf, this time did you bring one? (Adolf shakes head, Pina covers face again and opens) Adolf, did you bring one?

Adolf: No. Pina, now is not the time for this.

Pina: I remember that day in flower valley, you spoke of how beautiful the roses were. You said next time we meet, you would bring one for me from aboveground. I have waited so many years.

Adolf: After I returned aboveground, many things happened. (long pause) But now is not the time for this. Hurry and tell the elders to lead everyone in escaping up north.

Pina: (shakes head) Why do you not tell them yourself? I am

only waiting for a rose, not a message.

Adolf: Pina, what has gotten into you? This is a matter of life and death.

Pina: Then why do you not go yourself?

Adolf: I can't leave the army camps for too long. Rushing into your village will only cause unnecessary disputes and delays.

Pina: I took you back once, now I can take you back again.

Adolf: Pina, I must leave.

Pina: You must deliver this message to them yourself. Just like when I took you back and let them decide on your life and death.

Adolf: Why can I not ask you to deliver on my behalf? Our time is limited.

Pina: Because I am only responsible for bringing the person in front of them, not to announce a message. That was the case last time. This time is the same.

Adolf: The aboveground society in developing underground mineral and energy has issued many commands. They have already launched a full fled massacre and seizure. Our time is really running out.

Pina: We don't have any resources here. Could there really be no
way of any negotiating? You are supposed to be a civilized
society aboveground.

Adolf: No, there can't be.

Pina: Then take me to the person in charge? Maybe I could take
a letter of plea from the elders to beg for peace.

Adolf: I can't, because the current tactic is to wipe out the
underground and begin explorations of resources.

Pina: Don't tell me you can't! Take me to see the highest ranking
leader in charge of this tactic. If we don't try, how will we
know?

Adolf: No need.

Pina: Why?

Adolf: Because that man is standing before you.

Pina: Only you are standing before me. A chap in charge of
bringing a rose.

Adolf: Pina, after returning aboveground I was put away in an
insane asylum for many years. They said the country had no
underground, everyone did not believe me. Later the highest
level of government believed me. They took me out of the
asylum and thought highly of me. Can you understand my

predicament?

Pina: I will not convey anything on your behalf. If you want, go yourself.

Adolf: Pina, please don't make this more difficult for me that it already is. You were all once so good to me.

Pina: Then give me a rose!

Adolf: Stop bring up the damn rose!

Pina: I have not been waiting for a massacre either! (long pause) Let us start over. Adolf, many years no see! You have finally brought a rose for me? (Adolf shakes head) Hurry and say yes, you have brought a rose for me. I just want a rose, I don't want anything else.

Adolf: Then it is a shame what I bring is not a rose.

Pina: I don't want anything else. I don't want a spoken letter or message. "She is the Pina that allowed the underground to be discovered!" "She is the one who allowed someone from aboveground to live in our nation!" "South district has fallen. When will it be our turn? This is all Pina's doing!" We shall not alienate, everyone! We shall not be angered, everyone! We shall not dispute, everyone! So that is why everyone has taken the roses I have rolled, so well, and cut

them to shreds, thrown them to the ground. So, that is why everyone pretends I don't exist. You left, so easily you left, and it never occurred to you what misery awaited for who you left behind. Every single day, I must endure such agony! (long pause) So, all I wish for is a rose.

Adolf: I am very sorry, Pina. I really can't stay any longer. I beg of you, please tell everyone to quickly escape! I am so sorry.

(Adolf leaves)

Pina: My favorite, the rose.

(Adolf stops)

Adolf: Like fresh blood.

Pina: And their thorns.

Adolf: Like dried bones. I am so sorry.

(Adolf leaves)

Pina: I will not convey anything. I am just waiting for that rose.

(Lights of bombing and killings, music as loud as a tsunami-like influx, Pina stands motionless. Sudden silence)

(Song)
<Unblossomed flower>
My most beloved rose

Has not blossomed yet

(lights go out)

Frozen to Death

Adolf: Spring.

Pina: Moss begins to germinate on rocks. Sunshine fills the valley rendering a scene of luscious vegetation. Oh, and birds flying in to build their nests. Mother says the valley is dangerous. You can easily be seen. Actually, there are still many people who sneak off to play there.

Adolf: And flowers.

Pina: Flowers. Our flowers look as if they were splattered with little bitty dots of assorted paint. Teeny tiny specs expanding all over the burrow.

Adolf: Different from aboveground.

Pina: (right after Adolf) Different from aboveground. You say there are palm-sized lotuses aboveground, lilies like blares of trumpets, color conflicting wild pansies, a variety of flowers flourishing, each proudly and freely on display, coloring the entire Earth...... and my favorite, the rose.

Adolf: Spring.

Pina: Spring. Moss begins to germinate on rocks. Sunshine fills the valley rendering a scene of luscious vegetation. Oh, and birds flying in to build their nests. Mother says the valley is dangerous. You can easily be seen. Actually, there are still many people who sneak off to play there.

Adolf: And flowers.

Pina: My favorite, the rose.

Adolf: Your flowers look as if they were splattered with little bitty dots of assorted paint. Teeny tiny specs expanding all over the burrow.

Pina: Different from aboveground.

Adolf: And your favorite, the rose.

Pina: Red, covering the entire garden.

Adolf: Like fresh blood.

Pina: And their thorns.

Adolf: Like dried bones.

Pina: My favorite...... spring. Moss begins to germinate on rocks. Sunshine fills the valley rendering a scene of luscious vegetation. Oh, and birds flying in to build their nests. Mother says the valley is dangerous. You can easily be seen.

Actually, there are still many people who sneak off to play there.

Adolf: Sneak off to play there.

Pina: Sneak off to play there. The grassland is like Earth's green carpet, unlike the yellow sharp uneven gravel of the ground. Even after the soles of our feet are covered with callouses, we can still feel the softness from under them.

Adolf: I can almost feel the softness from under our feet now

Pina: The softness from under our feet, and the games being played using leaves.

Adolf: Using leaves to fold into small boats......

Pina: Using leaves to fold into spoons......

Adolf: Using leaves to make whistling sounds......

Pina: Shhh! (laughs) Mother says the valley is dangerous. You can easily be seen. This way we're going to be heard.

Adolf: Still many people sneak off to play there.

Pina: My favorite...... spring. Moss begins to germinate on rocks. Sunshine fills the valley rendering a scene of luscious vegetation.

Adolf: And your favorite, the rose.

Pina: Red, covering the entire garden.

Adolf: Like fresh blood.

Pina: And their thorns.

Adolf: Like dried bones.

Pina: And my favorite, the rose.

(Song)

Spring

Oh

Sneaking out to play, spring

Retina filled with green

Spring

Passionately grow

Full of joy

Oh

Spring

Adolf: And the rancid smell coming from the depth of the cave.

(music, lights change)

Adolf: Rancid smell coming from the depth of the cave.

(Pina does not smell anything)

Adolf: Rancid smell.

(long pause)

Adolf: Rancid.

(silence)

Adolf: Rancid. You once told that story.

Pina: (long pause) That was no story.

Adolf: But it left a deep impression on me, early spring the air would be filled with a rancid smell.

Pina: (smiling) The underground world is unbearable in the summer heat. In order to avoid the scorching heat, people packed lightly and traveled down along natural cave. As these cooler places gradually became more crowded and warmer, people continued to travel down and even further down in order to enjoy cool and comfortable temperatures. So, people forgot about the hot summer above and in a blink of an eye autumn arrives. Some people leave, but some are reluctant to leave the comfortable temperatures of the deep burrows. We would always prepare an abundant amount of food.

Adolf: But when autumn turns to winter, there is always a day when the temperature plummets, and unpredictably strong and freezing winds blow in from the North Pole. Those who

do not make it up in time would quickly freeze to death. Their bodies frozen, only to thaw and rot the coming springtime, creating the rancid rotting stench that fills the spring air.

Pina: And the caves are decorated with colorful flowers in full bloom. Skeletons and bones cannot hinder the determination to climb down. People step over bones to cooler places.

Adolf: To get through a hot summer it is better to just find a comfortable place to go. Even if one does not escape the north wind in time, they would be frozen to death within a few seconds anyway. That is what you told me.

Pina: That is what most people say.

Adolf: What about you?

Pina: I still remember during one of the autumn to winter seasons, in the depths of the cave; Great Aunt in faraway suddenly shouted .

Adolf: The north wind is coming.

Pina: Great Aunt was never really right in the head to start with, but fortunately she had a most filial daughter—every summer taking her down into the burrow, but she was very rowdy which made everyone nervous.

Great Aunt: The north wind is coming.

Pina: Great Aunt, there is no north wind.

Great Aunt: The north wind is coming.

Pina: Where is Aunty? Why did she let you run out on your own? Go back to your cave.

Great Aunt: The north wind is coming. Sister Moss has been frozen. Sister Moss has been frozen.

Pina: Oh, I understand. Aunty was sleeping and you snuck out.

Great Aunt: Run for your lives, the north wind is coming. Baby girl, hurry, run.

Pina: Great Aunt, I will take you back to Aunty.

(Pina took Great Aunt back in the other direction)

Great Aunt: Where is Fruehling?

Pina: Mother? She went up a bit to buy something.

Great Aunt: Quick, run! Let us go find your mother.

Pina: Great Aunt, wait a moment. Everyone is getting nervous. (toward all four directions) Everything is alright, do not worry, she is a bit out of her mind.

(a sharp and violent rumbling coming from far to near)

Great Aunt: (pushes Pina to the ground) Run for your lives! (Great Aunt is instantly frozen)

Pina: That is when I found out the north wind was like a block of white wall. The moment it hits someone, they harden. Someone stuck their head out to see Great Aunt's commotion and their head froze...... then when their legs went limp, their head hit the ground like a splattered watermelon. I ran, bewilderedly ran upwards. When I saw my mother, I grabbed her and continued to climb up all the way to a secure layer. There was a group like us who fled here in panic. We watched as the frosty north wind swept below us freezing all that did not escape in time, some frozen on stairs, some stuck mid-path. Where merely gusts of north wind grew stronger and stronger until the entire burrow was a sheet of white. A chill swept up. We were shiver while crying. Some cried out to the Earth and sky, sobbing, wailing until they passed out and were carried away. Some just sat on the side not saying a word. And a few, before everyone had a chance to react, jumped into the cave. Next thing you hear is usually glass breaking of some sort. (long pause) Then we each went back to our own homes and spent all winter mourning the dead.

Adolf: That makes you fear the burrow.

Pina: (shaking her head) Next summer, my family and I will
return to the burrow to avoid the summer heat.

Adolf: Next spring, Great Aunt will have become a rancid smell.

(Pina noncommittally shrugs shoulders, lights go out)

Interlude: Fetal Movement

(Pina curls up lying in a pool of blood. Man sits by the pool gently kicking water, rippling. After a long time, Pina slightly swings her elbow stretching all four limbs until she sits up. Pina sits in a pool of blood. Man sits by the pool gently kicking water, rippling. After a long time, Pina curiously and slowly looks around and stands up. Man sits by the pool gently kicking water, rippling. After a long time, Pina, with full gratitude, solemnly moves forward to the front edge of the pool. Man sits by the pool gently kicking water.)

Man: Pina, you are still here. You have not moved anywhere.

(long pause, lights dim)

Concentration Camp

(the man quietly changes into a different outfit and returns to Pina's side, Pina sitting still eyes looking straight ahead)

Sasha: His name is Lahong.

Pina: Who?

Sasha: The one that just got dragged away.

Pina: Mhm.

Sasha: His daughter has had a serious case of diarrhea these past few days.

Pina: Whose daughter?

Sasha: Lahong's daughter. He was caught stealing medicine from the clinic for his child.

Pina: Mhm.

Sasha: He will have his arms and legs cut off and placed in water to drown to death.

Pina: Really?

Sasha: Glanz Luo in bed 19, Geld Yuan in bed 23, Moss Xiu in

bed 36, Spring Gras in bed 41, Licht Mei in bed 44 and Mei Wasser in bed 53 all fell asleep last night and never woke up again.

Pina: (slightly tilts head) You know everything.

Sasha: Chong Stein in bed 6 and Bach Chang in bed 83 were discovered digging a secret escape route together.

Pina: So I have heard.

Sasha: (slightly raises eyebrow) Heard? (nonchalantly) They have been hanging in the square alive since the day before yesterday by a metal hook pierced through shoulder blades. They cursed the brutality of the society aboveground up until their last breath. Did you pass the square? Everyone just turned a blind eye and continued working, why?

Pina: Because we have been taught not to alienate.

Sasha: Yes.

(silence)

Sasha: Yesterday, the people of sector C secretly wanted to move our food, but were caught by Blume Yang in bed 57. She was shouting for everyone to come catch the thieves. Kristall Stone in bed 92 was also angered and yelling along with Blume Yang at the people of sector C, but I do not

know why the people of sector C were so daring to continue moving all our rations straight towards sector C. Blume Yang furiously ran up to stop them while shouting for others to come judge the situation. Did you know about this?

Pina: I was there.

Sasha: People of Sector C cowardly said, "We did not steal, we did not steal," while pushing aside Blume Yang's hand. Although Section C's movements are not big, ultimately they have more people. Relying on just the two of them alone, how can they possibly block them? Kristall Stone was furious and yelled out, "We already do not have enough food to eat! Why do you allow them to blatantly take our food supply for tomorrow?" Nobody spoke a word. Blume Yang roared with anger, "Everyone, come and help! Save your own portion of food! Save your own portion of food! Save your own portion of food!" (pause) Seeing what the quiet circle of observers now becoming a little agitated, Kristall Stone quickly grabbed a barrel of food and started yelling, "Quick! Come help!" A few others started yelling and rushed up to lend a hand. Sector C may have many people, but with others blocking them, naturally they would

not be able to successfully take away the food barrels. In the midst of confusion someone knocked over half a barrel of food. (pause) Then bang, bang, bang! Gunshots! Kristall Stone, Blume Yang and their helpers were all shot to death. Meanwhile when hearing the gunshots, the people of Sector C silently laid face down on the ground. So, no one was hit by a single bullet. Then they silently got up from the ground, silently lifted the rice and vegetables barrels and silently left. When I arrived at the scene, they had all fallen to the ground. The crowds were still there, but no one came forth to help them shut their eyes. I heard someone ask, "Just let them take it, why lose a life over it?" Another asked, "This was all because they were too rowdy, why did they not just report to the supervisor?" Someone also asked, "No disputing, you see, is this not just due retribution?" And another even said, "What a waste of half a barrel of food."

(looks at Pina, Pina realizes she is being stared at)

Pina: (panics and touches her own face) Something wrong?

(Sasha shakes head)

Sasha: I was grinding my teeth, all the while tears dripped endlessly. I walked forward to help Kristall Stone and others

cover their wide opened eyes. I was so enraged, so enraged. So I stood staring at them in a pool of blood among the crowds of people, viciously, as if I wanted to beat their faces with my glare. They were all frightened, some took a few steps back, some did not know what to do, and then I heard amongst the crowd someone whispering......

Pina: No anger.

Sasha: Yes, no anger. Originally, this was a very soft voice. Then the second person said it, then a third, then everybody started chanting at the same volume and tempo gently, saying to me, "No anger, no anger, no anger......" as if getting angry was my mistake. (pause) The supervisor has arrived, leading the workers to dispose of each corpse one at a time. The crowd dispersed, leaving me standing there alone.

Sasha: How do you feel?

Pina: (shakes head) I feel very upset .

Sasha: (laughs) I am upset, as well. In the midst of that crowd maybe there were people who were also feeling upset, but they still dispersed and went about their own businesses. Even the blood was covered with a layer of dirt and ashes,

nothing was left.

Pina: I know.

(Sasha shakes head, lights change, singer performs "You do not know")

Suffering of hunger

Beauty of being full

How do you not know

Death, you know

Destruction, you know

You use your mouth to recite many times

You use your eyes to read many times

But you have never experienced for yourself

If the homes did not crumble before you

Then how would you know that pain

I personally have no pain or injuries

You are willing to know

Tears keep falling and falling

Turning and continuing to smile and ignore

You really know?

Then what is the next step
Do you know?
You know or you don't know
You know
or you don't know

(lights change)

Sasha: Do you know who I am?

Pina: I'm sorry. I don't.

Sasha: Never mind (pause) I have memorized all the people on the camp T list. Lately Camp I and Camp P have started killing each other.

Pina: I am not really clear about that.

(Pina leaves but Sasha grabs her hand)

Sasha: I know who you are. (Pina freezes) So, come chat with me.

(Pina quietly sits back in her original seat)

Pina: Who are you?

Sasha: I would like to finish the story of Camp I and Camp P, may I? (Pina noncommittally shrugs shoulders) Have you

heard of what happened to these two camps?

Pina: I am not sure.

Sasha: Try to tell me. Let me know how much you understand.

Pina: (thinking for a moment) A senior official ordered Camp I and Camp P to be merged……

Sasha: So, Camp I and Camp P began killing each other over limited resources and larger activity space, right?

Pina: Yes.

Sasha: Whose fault do you think it is?

Pina: I do not know.

Sasha: Camp I was the first to be dug up from the underground and persecuted. They should know best the feeling of being oppressed and slaughtered. Now they just continue to treat Camp P with the same brutality whether in the underground or here. People really never learn their lessons.

Pina: I don't know why you are telling me all this.

Sasha: The children of Camp P painfully cried: "The safest place is our graves." Then why are we still alive?

Pina: (becoming uneasy) I wish to leave.

Sasha: Do you remember Lahong?

Pina: The one that had arms and legs cut off and thrown in a

pool after caught stealing.

Sasha: The one who had no choice but to steal medicine to heal his daughter. (pause) Before he was taken away, he begged me to take care of his child. I asked him, "Life is already too painful, why not just let the child die?" Do you know how he replied? (Pina shakes her head) Because he believed that this child one day, one day would be able to live an ordinary, happy life. And for that day, he must let her live. Do you think this child will see such a day?

Pina: I don't know.

Sasha: Then will the senior officials know?

Pina: What?

Sasha: What do you think is simple happiness?

Pina: What senior officials?

Sasha: I think simple happiness is to be with those you love, to not be subject to "no alienating, no disputing, no anger," to completely be yourself, to leave concentration camp, maybe even the underground, to live a life of free choice.

Pina: What senior officials were you talking about?

Sasha: It does not matter whether we are in the underground or in concentration camp; we still are regulated and constrained.

There's no difference. They are different only in level, one is harsher, the other is milder. Do you feel it?

(Pina shakes head)

Sasha: This is why we have fallen into such a state. Pina, I know who you are. You are the one who allowed Adolf to survive.

Pina: I did not.

Sasha: You said let everyone decide on his life or death, but then used the teachings of the elders to grant him survival. (pause) I also know he lived with your family for a period of time, is this true? (Pina is silent, Sasha appears agitated) So it was you. It really was you……

Pina: What are you doing?

Sasha: I will not do anything to you. (laughs) No anger, right? (laughs, then repeats "no anger" as a chant until returning to previous state), my home region, I heard, was rich in mine, so originally the whole region of people were directly thrown in the river to be washed away after being purged. However, the number of people thrown in the river was really too many, the river almost stuck. My mother and I were back from visiting relatives. We walked up the river and only to see it stained of red and clogged with corpses

colliding. With one glance, I found my father amongst them. Then we were brought here by the soldiers and beyond our expectation, we survived.

Pina: I have heard your story, may I go now?

Sasha: No, I will leave after you have listen to my request.

Pina: Go ahead.

Sasha: I know Senior Official Adolf has been trying to find you again. I also know you have been trying to avoid being found, because you wish to expiate your guilt. So, I demand that you to be found by Senior Official Adolf and for them to take me away along with Lahong's child.

Pina: This……

Sasha: Did you not wish to expiate your guilt?

(Pina hesitates)

Sasha: For this child to live a simple, happy life, I want you to contact Senior Official Adolf.

Pina: (hesitates) Fine, I know what to do.

Sasha: Thank you. I await your notice. My name is Sasha. (about to exits) Oh, by the way, is your mother still alive?

Pina: Yes.

Sasha: Hope you can fathom the loss of a mother. The woman,

Blume Yang, who was shot to death while stopping Sector C from stealing food, was my mother, did you know?

(Sasha exits, light change)

(Song)
Oh~
Storm of knowledge
You know right from wrong
Questions of emotions
Who can answer them
Do not say you know
You only know the surface
Empathy too insincere
Experience too contrived
Pity too haughty
Do not say you know
Our pain only we ourselves fully understand
All the words in the world are useless

Let you be me, experience my inner storm
Let you be me, so you may not only mourn the surface

If you knew

Do not speak anymore

Just one embrace

Stone Tower

Mother: Baby girl, more fallen people have been discovered near the west gate. You have been going there quite frequently lately. I am very worried......

Pina: Mother......

Mother: If you see a person from aboveground......

Pina: I must use stones to strike them unconscious, making sure they have blacked out and immediately report back, correct?

Mother: You know very well, but it is very hard for you to actually do it.

Pina: I know.

Mother: You have no idea, baby girl, you have no idea. You have overly simplified the situation. They are living people. When you strike their bodies with stone after stone, they will cry in pain and beg for mercy. Maybe you will smash them until they are black and blue, but they are still conscious. You must knock them unconscious by striking

their bodies with stone after stone. You must strike until their brains splatter, you must do it! You must not relent! You must not relent! You must not relent!

Pina: Must we be so barbaric?

Mother: Baby girl! You do not understand how savage the aboveground people are, so please do not accuse your own clansmen of being barbaric. They slaughtered us, forcing us underground to live in such tight quarters. But they are still frantically searching for us. They have filled every cave that remotely resembles any gateway we may use, forever blocking our sunlight. Some say, other countries condemn how cruel the people aboveground have treated the people underground. Yet the people aboveground deny the existence of the undergrounds. Baby girl, currently the underground world may be comfortable and suitable for living, but we cannot forget the painful and tragic history that the people aboveground have brought upon us.

Pina: I will not forget.

(Song)

Stone tower, stone tower

Pick up a stone and pile it up

Fill any holes on it

Be careful, be careful

Dirty things will fall down

Falling to the ground with a bang

If

Still panting, still moving

Then

Let the stones fly, let the stones smash

Never become tired of throwing stones

If something is heard, stop, stop and ignore

Let the stones fly, pile the stones up

Until only a pile of stones is left, bang bang bang

Never become tired of throwing stones

Pick up a stone and pile it up

Stone tower, stone tower

Pina: Mother, have the elders taught us no disputing, no
alienating, no anger? (pause) But why have we sung such a
terrifying song since childhood?

Mother: When you treat someone wholeheartedly, are you sure they will treat you the same way?

Pina: Not necessarily.

Mother: Especially the savage people aboveground.

Pina: So we must obliterate them from the start? Aaron from the East Cave beats and scolds his wife from time to time. He cheats and he steals. Why don't we stone him to death?

Mother: He is one of the underground people, so he will not commit any heinous crimes.

Pina: Even if he throws his children to their deaths?

Mother: Aaron said it was an accident.

Pina: Will children accidentally fall and break their heads open? He clearly is violent to his children.

Mother: No alienating.

(pause)

Pina: Mother! Why, now, are you silencing me again with the teachings of our elders?

Mother: No disputing.

(Pina explodes with resentment)

Mother: No anger.

(Pina suppresses for a while, finally like a deflating ball,

drops her shoulders)

Aaron from the East Cave beats and scolds his wife from time
   to time. He cheats and steals. Why do we not stone him to
   death?

Mother: He is one of the underground people. He will not
   commit any heinous crimes.

Pina: Even if he throws his children to their deaths?

Mother: Aaron said it was an accident.

Pina: Will children accidentally fall and break their heads open?
   He clearly is violent to his children.

Mother: No alienating.

(pause)

Pina: Mother! Why, at moments like these, are you silencing me
   again with the teachings of our elders?

Mother: No disputing.

(long pause)

Mother: No anger.

(Pina feels oppressed)

Pina: Even if he throws his children to their deaths?

Mother: Aaron said it was an accident.

Pina: Will children accidentally fall and break their heads open?

He clearly is violent to his children.

Mother: No alienating.

(pause)

Pina: Mother! Why, at moments like these, are you silencing me again with the teachings of our elders?

Mother: No disputing.

(pause)

Mother: No anger.

(pause)

Pina: Mother, I just wonder if we don't talk about cause and effect, how should we learn and progress.

Mother: Discussion does not necessarily bring progress. Do your own fair share of things. People say, "the front man is always exposed to attack." Remember, never rush to the frontline in any situation. A beating awaits anyone who rushes quickly to the front. Leave decision for others to make, as much as possible. And don't fall too behind or you will be eliminated at any chance.

Pina: Then what if everyone all stay in the middle?

Mother: Then there will not be anyone to lead us—to lead us in the wrong path causing us to be beaten, no one will bring

danger.

(silent)

Pina: Mother, I have brought back a man from aboveground…

… his name is Adolf.

(lights go out)

Interlude: Nonsense

Pina: (gasps) Hoo hoo hoo, hah shih!

A: Can you help me pass that?

Pina: Which one?

B: The snail's jogging shoes.

Pina: Stars (same pronunciation as gorilla)

C: Hanging on the pointer, do you see?

A: That is a gorilla.

B: What about the snail's jogging shoes?

A: They are in the 9th drawer on the left.

C: There won't be a happy ending.

Pina: Because of "nine?"

A: Yes, because of "nine." No nine will have a happy ending.

C: Repeat after me. "shout!"

Pina: Shout.

A: Why do you shout?

Pina: Why shout?

D: Lions can't get their bananas, and they are angry.

E: We need elephant's webs.

F: So sorry, today's elephant has no webs.

Pina: Then I will take a tail.

No tail.

No reason.

No death.

A: Can you help me pass that?

Pina: Which one?

B: The snail's jogging shoes.

A: It is not.

A: Can you help me pass that?

Pina: Which one?

A: Your life.

Pina: I can't.

(lights go out)

Self Introduction

(Initially, Adolf brings out from the side a microphone with a stand, Pina is in good posture)

Adolf: Adolf.

Pina: Pina.

Adolf: I am already dead.

Pina: I do not know if I am living or dead.

Adolf: When I was 32, I took a gun, aimed it at my own temple and killed myself.

Pina: When I was 33, Helena, Sasha and I returned to our homes underground. (to Adolf) Why did you kill yourself?

Adolf: Because I chose to, because you were all afraid to choose.

Pina: Mhm…… actually, we had no choice. Since we had no choice, it was better to adapt.

Adolf: So no right to choose applies for all things?

Pina: Yes.

(long pause)

Adolf: (sighs) I am Adolf, from Xu Na. I was the first person to discover the underground world, reside in it, and receive government training. I became the highest executive in the underground development department at age 26, making me the youngest high level minister in history. In addition to ensuing the ultimate goal of "Developing the Underground for New Resources," I also supported the "Disease Control Department" for pathology research and related experiments, providing the "National Construction and Development Department" with related manpower. (Proudly) I respected and followed the instructions of my seniors to allow advanced progress and development for our nation as the primary objective. I fully executed policies of underground development, maximizing the benefits of the country as a main goal. The country's success is my personal success. (long pause, to Pina) Do you understand that the country takes priority over everything?

Pina: Mhm...... that's all fine by me.

(silence)

Adolf: Do you believe in salvation?

Pina: What?

Adolf: Do you hold hatred? Towards the society aboveground?

Pina: If there is no choice, then what can be done of our hatred?

Adolf: What about revenge?

Pina: Eh?...... That is something we dare not think about. How do we make the entire aboveground society the enemy?

Adolf: So you choose mercy? If, back then, the underground had launched a protest, perhaps you would now still be living safely there.

Pina: But...... we were dug up from the underground, were we not?

Adolf: (agitated) Then why when being dug up did you not put up a fight?

Pina: (thinking) So we can only live together with death.

Adolf: Even now?

Pina: (laughs) Even now I feel death is breathing by my ear.

Adolf: And I am the farmer spreading the seeds of death.

Pina: You have been most diligent.

Adolf: Yes, I have been most diligent.

Pina: (laughs) Everyone says, "Concentration camp has no God, because this is a place so horrible that even God has also

decided not to come."

Adolf: Seems like my diligence has gained an unprecedented victory.

Pina: Yes.

(silence)

Adolf: Does Sasha hate you? Because I often ask you to come see me?

Pina: I try my best, try my best not to let her hate me.

Adolf: Should be very difficult.

Pina: But…… we only have each other left.

Adolf: Pina, how can you be so…… at ease?

Pina: Probably because I didn't speak up when I could, so now I can only accept.

Adolf: Are you able to accept anything?

Pina: (long pause) Yes, I think so. It can't get much worse. I have been in concentration camp. I've seen a son beat his father to death over a piece of bread. I've seen people stampede other people to death, frantically dodging gunshots. Living and dying are not much different, both are fine.

Adolf: Looks like the concentration camp has been run well.

Pina: Yes.

(long pause)

Adolf: What if, back then, I did not find you in the concentration camp?

Pina: Then I would probably be buried underground with my mother.

Adolf: Now that you have accidentally survived, do you hate me?

Pina: No, I can only focus on the present. The past and future are both things I do not have the ability to think about.

Adolf: Pina, you hate me, don't you? Please tell me the truth.

Pina: Senior Official Adolf, I only think about what work might need to be done next. Love and hate are not in my control.

Adolf: Senior Official Adolf? You called me, Senior Official Adolf……! Fine, I order you to answer me! You hate me.

(silence)

Adolf: You hate me?

(silence, Pina deep in thought)

Pina: Mr. Adolf, I only think about what work might need to be done next. Love and hate are not in my control.

Adolf: Can this make your hatred disappear?

Pina: I don't know.

Adolf: But you hate me? (Pina continues to think, long pause) All of the underground people spurn me?

Pina: I can't speak for them.

Adolf: But you also can't speak for yourself.

Pina: (thinking) Then death is the only solution?

Adolf: At least I chose! The way I see it, all the burden has been dumped on me, because those who should have made decisions hesitated to do so. It's really very pathetic, all those afraid to make decisions. (Walks in front of microphone) I am Adolf.

(Pina hesitates, presses her lips together and sighs, staring off into space as lost if in thought. Suddenly, Adolf takes the microphone and shoves it towards Pina's mouth. Pina turns away. Their actions gradually grow violent until Adolf gives up and returns the microphone to its stand. Lights fade until completely dark, Pina finally walks to the microphone, tapping it gently. Lights back on.)

Pina: (weakly) I am Pina.

(lights wait, realizing Pina does not continue to speak, lights go out)

Interlude : Mother Said

A: Pina.

Pina: Mother? Are you Mother?

Mother: Yes, I am Mother. Are you doing well?

Pina: Mother, I am doing very well.

Mother: Pina, do you remember what I told you?

Pina: I remember you told me about the last three days. (long
pause)

Pina: Mother, are you still there?

Mother: Pina, do you remember what I told you?

Pina: Mother told me that the last three days, all the loved ones
would come back to my side to reevaluate my life and
remake decisions.

Mother: Pina, do you remember what I told you?

Pina: Mother, on the last three days the voices of loved ones
will appear?

Mother: Pina, do you remember what I told you?

Pina: Mother, how will I know the last three days have come?

Mother: Pina, do you remember what I told you??

Pina: Mother, have you already been born by Mother Earth into the new world?

Mother: Pina, do you remember what I told you??

Pina: Mother, have you seen Great Aunt and Aunty?

Mother: Pina, do you remember what I told you??

Pina: Mother, everyone is doing well there?

Mother: Pina, do you remember what I told you??

Pina: Mother, my last three days have come?

Mother: Pina, do you remember what I told you??

Pina: Mother, are we going to remake all the decisions?

Mother: Pina, do you remember what I told you??

Pina: Mother, only you have come?

Mother: Pina, do you remember what I told you??

Pina: Mother, how should I prepare for the last three days?

Mother: Pina, why did you not kill Adolf?

Pina: Mother, we are starting to…… ?!

Mother: Pina, do you remember what I told you?? Why didn't you kill Adolf?

(silence, Pina tries calling for Mother a few times)

Pina: Mother? (long pause) Mother? (long pause) Mother, when will my last three days come? (silence) Mother?

A: I am Adolf.

(lights go out)

Finale

(Pina arbitrarily waves her hand. The man is making unidentifiable movements like water that is about to boil. Music is chaotic and blasting, multifocal scene.)

Man: Adolf! The red rose I have been waiting for is like fresh blood with thorns like bones. The ground has no stars. Mother's eyes have no stars, only crimson-dyed streams and floating corpses. I can see right away that you are a cow, why do you not run from me?

Pina: Silence!

Man: Because I am waiting for a rose. Childish! Mr. Adolf, childish! Mr. Adolf, the north wind is here, baby girl! Tonight, would you like to have roasted cuisses de grenouille or the rotten head I have thrown on the ground?

Pina: The red one.

Man: A palm sized lotus hits upon the corpse. I will take care of

you and Helena. Parasite! Quickly escape with your clansmen riding white snails through the thick smoke to become thin little flowers on rock walls then being scraped off.

Pina: Mother.

Man: Like a robot. Just like a robot eating a lollipop. For survival, waving flags and shouting on the side, watching Camp I and Camp P madly shooting cannons into each other. Propelling the knocked over bucket of food into the body, sucking them out through a vacuum, slowly turning. Do you see me? Slowly turning in the dark. Hurry and find me.

Pina: Mother, you still have not told me……

Man: Sir, whitefish, Sir, cuisses de grenouille, Sir, Adolf, I am waiting only for a single rose. I'd rather live for a piece of candy, like the waves of an underground lake. Lahong, Lahong! Your child, your child. I don't know if they're living a simple life of happiness. Mother, Mother, you're my child……

Pina: Mother, when will my last three days come?

Man: Don't be afraid. Before you decide, all your dear friends who are one step ahead of you and have already been born by Mother Earth will return to your side. Use three days'

time. The last three days they will accompany you in remaking your decision. Really? We're all in the womb of Mother Earth. We're just in the womb of Mother Earth waiting to be born. Prior to this, we must endlessly reflect on what is right and wrong and reevaluate all the decisions that came from emotions. When we finally make the purest decision, that is when we will make our way down the birth canal of Mother Earth and enter into a whole new world. Is this true? I don't know. Is this true? I don't know. Is this true? Have you made a choice? Have you made a decision? Do you dare to choose? Do you dare to decide? Mother? Mother? Don't leave me here...... how will the last three days come?

Pina: Don't say anymore.

(sudden silence followed by extreme calm and neutral dialogue)

Man: Why are you stopping me?

Pina: I don't want you to say anymore.

Man: Why not?

Pina: No disputing, no alienating, no anger.

Man: Why not?

Pina: I don't know.

Man: You don't know, so you bring disaster back to the underground world.

Pina: This is a decision everyone made together.

Man: Because you didn't want to take responsibility, which led to everyone being slaughtered or sent to concentration camp. Only Sasha is left. You and Helena were sent back underground. Your clansmen have all died, because you did nothing.

Pina: I did! I sent out a warning. I once tried to escape. I participated in protest.

Man: You only hide yourself inside.

Pina: Then what should I do?

Man: Yes, what should you do?

Pina: Find the source of guilt.

Man: Who?

Pina: Adolf. This is all your fault.

Man: My fault?

Pina: Your fault.

Man: So, allowing myself to survive is my own fault? Not notifying clansmen to escape north is my fault? Not fully supporting Sasha's fight for the right to remain aboveground

is my fault? Not setting aside time to talk with Helena about beautiful memories is also my fault? Your relatives are all dead, the country is destroyed, all my fault.

Pina: Yes! All your fault.

Man: Then what are you going to do?

Pina: Kill Adolf. (Pina cold-bloodedly picks up the knife and frantically stabs the man, the blood instantly sprays like a fountain.)

Man: (laughing) It hurts. Pina, it hurts.

Man: Why not try to really kill me (peels off safety film from knife, hacks surrounding object to prove sharpness of blade, then pushes the knife up against neck) like this?

Pina: Yes, go ahead and kill yourself.

(The man puts down the knife, looking straight at Pina. Pina tries a few moves, the man repeats. Pina suddenly comes to her senses and gives up.)

Man: Only you can kill yourself.

(Man returns to water)

Pina: (looking toward Sasha and Helena's skeletons) You won't come find me, will you? (Pina quietly makes a decision and walks back towards the depths of the cave,

lights slowly fade)

(Captions: Apparently, Pina saw a light in the depths of the cave. Mother Earth's new world welcomed her. Her mother and loved ones were all waiting there for her. They warmly welcomed her arrival with smiles and embraces. Sasha, Helena and Adolf were among them as well. Lights go out.)

The End

地下女子：穢土天堂二部曲

作　　　者／鍾伯淵
社　　　長／林宜澐
總　編　輯／廖志墘
英文翻譯／倪湘鈴
英文編校／游文綺
中文校對／江子逸
編輯協力／葉育伶、林韋聿
書籍設計／三人制創
內文排版／藍天圖物宣字社

出　　　版／蔚藍文化出版股份有限公司
　　　　　　地址：10667臺北市大安區復興南路二段237號13樓
　　　　　　電話：02-7710-7864　　傳真：02-7710-7868
　　　　　　臉書：https://www.facebook.com/AZUREPUBLISH/
　　　　　　讀者服務信箱：azurebks@gmail.com

總　策　畫／曉劇場 Shinehouse Theatre
　　　　　　地址：台北市萬華區環河南路二段125巷15弄21號
　　　　　　電話：0953-186-507
　　　　　　觀眾服務信箱：Shinehouse0820@gmail.com

總　經　銷／大和書報圖書股份有限公司
　　　　　　地址：24890新北市新莊市五工五路2號
　　　　　　電話：02-8990-2588

法律顧問／眾律國際法律事務所　　著作權律師／范國華律師
　　　　　　電話：02-2759-5585　　網站：www.zoomlaw.net

印　　　刷／世和印製企業有限公司
定　　　價／台幣280元

初版一刷／2017年11月
ISBN 978-986-94403-6-3

※欲利用本書全部或部份內容，請洽曉劇場 Shinehouse0820@gmail.com